Mafietta

DEDICATION

I'd just like to take a moment to say THANK YOU, to all of the strong women who made me who I am. . .

To my Mom Mom – thank you for showing me what it means to be a lady.

To my Grandma Creola - thank you for reminding me to always be who I AM.

To my Mom – thanks for always being there to listen.

To Brittany - Thank you for being there to offer your support and advice.

To Melinda – Thank you for ALWAYS being the wind beneath my wings!! I couldn't have made it without you.

AND TO MY WONDERFUL HUSBAND
– Thank you for being the man GOD created you to be and always encouraging me to pursue my dream. I know there is a place for us TOGETHER at the TOP!!!

Cover art – by Jason Wall

This is the number one rule for your set

In order to survive, gotta learn to live with regrets

On the, rise to the top, many drop, don't forget

In order to survive, gotta learn to live with regrets

This is the number one rule for your set

In order to survive, gotta learn to live with regrets

If through our travels we get separated, never forget

In order to survive, gotta learn to live with regrets

Chorus to Jay-Z song

"Regrets"

From the *Reasonable Doubt* Album

When my children ask me how I did it, I tell them I watched the mistakes of those that came before me. Then I used their mistakes to create the playbook that took our family to the top.

Up until our time, many were the stories of kingpins turned inmates. Most often, the girlfriends, mistresses, and wives who survived the experience were lost once their man was shipped away on a forced vacation. This would not be me.

I turned this paradigm on its head. I turned trouble season into double season.

Take Me to the King

Part 1

You could know someone your whole life and never know what they really want to be or what their real dream is. You will never know their innermost desires. Some of them, they are afraid to speak to the Universe—and some of them, they are afraid of admitting to themselves …

Clarke

Thursdays were always the busiest day of the week at the office. I was executive assistant for Eric Smith, one of the most successful lawyers in the Port City. It was Thursday, and I was swamped with work, the same as every other Thursday. Eric always overbooked appointments on Thursdays so he could slip out early on Fridays and play golf with his frat brothers. As the clock struck five, I shut down my computer and grabbed my purse and then my cell phone to call my home girl, Tracy. It was ladies' night!

"What's up, Tracy? What you got going on, girl?" I said when she picked up. After taking calls all day in my professional mode, it was always good to loosen up and call her after work.

"Not a thing, girl. Deanna and I are just sitting here talking about going to the Sportsman Club tonight. You down?" I could hear Deanna in the background, talking loud as usual, and I was dreading the night already.

"Girl, you know I don't fool with her. She talks too much."

Tracy just laughed. She knew I didn't really care for Deanna, but she was her friend, so that made her an unwelcomed toleration for me.

"Girl, bye," she said. "You know she can't help it. Are you coming by on your way home?"

"Yeah, I'll grab a bottle and come by, but if she starts getting on my nerves—I'm out."

Twenty minutes later I was knocking on the door at Tracy's apartment. When Tracy opened the door, she looked like she was already ready to go out. She just stood at the door and posed, waiting on me to say something. She was wearing this skintight black dress. Both sides of it were sheer, and she was killing it with a pair of red pumps. Home girl looked good.

She had the perfect body and she knew it. I wouldn't dare put anything like that on. I was a size twelve. I know that's not too big, but I still wouldn't wear anything that short and revealing.

I stood there in the hallway and told her what was true—what she wanted to hear—so I could get through the door. I said, "Dang, girl, you killing them with that, but why in the world are you ready so early?" I asked. It was only about six o'clock.

"We ain't going nowhere right now," Tracy said. "I'm just trying it on. What I look like?" She knew she looked good; she just wanted me to stroke her ego as usual. I cut my eye at her and smiled as I made my way into her apartment.

Before I made it down the short hallway that led into her living room, I heard that irritating voice. Deanna was always running her mouth. She was always threatening to beat someone up or talking about some temper tantrum she'd just had. She was the true definition of a project chick. I'd learned to pretty much tune her out, so I was really amazed as I heard her describe the man she'd just met. It was some Jamaican dude who owned the Marley Grill on Castle Street. By the time she was finished, all our mouths were hanging open.

"Not those guys—they are too quiet," I said.

"Exactly, girl. They have to be quiet," Deanna responded. Then she went on and on about the weight they moved. These guys operated like the Mafia. They were the Bellows. This Mafia-style family was supposedly head up by a couple of brothers who were always surrounded by their enforcers. According to Deanna, they were the real deal. Most of the guys that surrounded them were nephews or other close cousins, and they didn't play around.

She went on and on about the moves they were making. Per Deanna's account of the family, they even had a fat guy named Scott who tracked, deposited, and invested all their money. These dudes were organized, and they were thorough.

Instantly I was intrigued. I wanted to be in that restaurant.

She said she met one of them in the club, and when he approached her, she flat out told him how ugly he was. She described him as being stocky and brown skinned with a wide face and big lips. She said the nigga actually laughed. He told her he knew that, but he wanted to take her home anyway. To hear her tell it, he just came out and told her that he wanted to sleep with her.

She decided to be just as bold with him and asked, "You got five hundred dollars?"

He pulled it out and threw it on the bar without even blinking. That was the first of many nights she would sleep with Admiral Bellow.

The rest of her conversation was about how many cars he had and how the business operated. According to her, these niggas had the kind of money that got them offshore accounts and homes in the islands. I didn't hear much of what she was saying after that. My mind was racing.

I wanted to live the lifestyle you see in the movies, but I refused to deal with another flunky—I wanted the *boss*. I was just coming off the high of a fifty-pound weight loss, and my self-esteem was through the roof. (What a difference fifty pounds could make!)

As exciting as it was, Deanna's personal account of this family was not good enough for me. I wanted to find out for myself. And I had a plan. I went out with Tracy and Deanna that night, but instead of dancing, I spent the evening thinking about the Bellows. I couldn't wait to get home so I could figure this thing out.

Butterflies had taken over my stomach by the time I woke up the next morning. I was energized and excited. I felt an adventure coming, and if I played this thing right, I would land my dream role.

The Chicken That Changed My Life

My first visit to Marley Grill took almost a day to plan. It wasn't just because I'd never eaten any more than a beef patty before; it was because I was excited to see what was behind the doors of that restaurant. My voice trembled as I called to place a simple order of jerk chicken with only white meat. I wanted to get to the bottom of Deanna's story, but it couldn't make me eat a chicken leg or thigh. I only liked white meat.

I was really nervous as I made the call. I was not prepared for the deep Jamaican accent that greeted me from the other side of the phone. I remember saying the words *please* and *thank you* like a million times. I wanted to stand out from the other women who called there to place orders. I wanted this order of chicken to change my life. I had to be *different*.

The Grill was less than ten minutes from my apartment, and I headed there as soon as I got off the phone. I was still dressed from work, so I was casually fly. The small restaurant was nestled between a strip mall and a church.

There were a few guys hanging out front when I pulled up. I'd always seen them hanging out there when I was passing by, but I never paid them any attention before. This time I noticed that each of them was wearing gold somewhere. Everybody's pants were hard creased and their sneakers were fresh. They were much cleaner than the average guys just hanging out on the corners around there.

I felt like I was in Jamaica as soon as I walked in the building. The music, color scheme, and smell of the food only fueled my curiosity. I liked the atmosphere. I walked to the cash register and waited.

There was a group of guys playing dominoes in the corner by the door and a bar on the right that spanned the length of the restaurant. The top of the wall behind the bar was covered in flags from other Caribbean islands. Mirrors covered the rest of the wall, except for a small corner that had pictures of a tall guy with a big smile with Bob Marley, Buju Banton, and another guy I didn't recognize.

A short, bald guy came from the kitchen and asked if he could help me. He was sort of stocky. I wondered if this was Scott, but I didn't know and I couldn't ask.

"I'd like to pick up my call-in order," I said.

"You had a call-in?" the guy asked.

"Yes, jerk chicken with only white meat."

"Hold on," he curtly replied.

He seemed to have an attitude as he dragged himself back to the kitchen. He was stocky and moved around lazily. This was definitely not the best customer service I'd experienced. I felt my visit was more of an intrusion than a welcomed activity.

A different guy came out of the kitchen with a white Styrofoam plate. He had to be at least six one. He wore a black shirt with bright-yellow letters that read "Marley Grill." There was one other guy wearing the same shirt; everyone else had on street clothes. The man opened the Styrofoam box. I looked inside and a cloud of steam hit my face. It smelled fantastic.

A full smile filled my face. I was excited about tasting the contents of that box. The smells coming from it were unfamiliar to me, but they activated my taste buds. As I picked up my head, he closed the box and told me it was $8.49.

I was sure to pay with the crisp twenty-dollar bill I'd gotten from the ATM earlier. Impressions were important. The wrong choice could send me further from the dream that I played over and over in my head. I had to be different from any other woman who came into that restaurant.

I knew I would be back as soon as I walked out of the front door. That interaction just wasn't going to cut it. I wanted to dine in next time. My pickup didn't give me the recon I needed to figure out who was who, so

I called Tracy. She was always comfortable in any situation and had no trouble making friends.

Two days later, we headed to the Grill. The same group of guys were in the corner playing dominoes again. Tracy sat at the bar, two seats away from the crowd, but I didn't want to do that. It made her look too eager, and I didn't want to play the game that way. I moved two seats below her, just so we appeared to be together, but in a way that distanced me from the group of men. I didn't even glance their way. I wasn't interested in them.

Moments later, the same tall, dark-skinned, full-lipped guy who opened the plate for me before emerged from the kitchen wearing a fresh, black shirt reading "Marley Grill" just as before. This time it was clear he was the one I wanted.

He was different from the other guys in there. He moved in a slow and quiet way that commanded attention. This dude had swag. He was the only one in the restaurant that seemed to be working, but you could tell he owned the place.

I looked over at Tracy. She had a conversation of her own going with a couple of the guys in the corner. There was no one there to be the buffer; I had to talk to this man myself. He seemed nice enough. He had the biggest, most innocent-looking eyes, and for a second, I could see myself reflected in them. This was the moment I discovered my love for Jamaican cuisine.

Tracy was familiar with a couple of the guys in the corner, so the conversation was lighthearted and easy for her, but this man had only asked me what I wanted to order, and my hands were already sweating. I didn't know a lot about Jamaican food, so I had to stick with my order from the other day.

"I'd like jerk chicken with white meat, cabbage, peas, and rice," I said.

"This is the same thing you got two days ago," the man said. I was surprised that he remembered that. I was taken aback, but felt accomplished.

Mission #1 completed: he had taken notice.

We made small talk about Jamaican food and its different flavors, but his flavor was the only one I had on my mind. I was intrigued by this man and that deep accent. I wanted to know more about him. When the check came this time, again I paid with a crisp twenty-dollar bill. He needed to see that I had my own money.

"You'll have to try something different the next time you come," he said.

"Nah, probably not," I replied in the sweetest voice I could muster. "This works for now. I'll have to take it slow. All of this is new to me."

The tall, dark man laughed and said, "Don't worry. I'll take my time with you." Then he walked into the kitchen.

I believe he got my drift, but he wasn't as engaged as I wanted him to be. I obviously had his attention, but he was keeping things strictly professional. I wanted to change the course of the conversation, but I wanted him to initiate whatever happened. My plan was moving along, but not as quickly as I'd hoped. I wasn't ready to give up, though.

A few days passed before we returned to the restaurant. This time I was greeted with a smile as I walked through the door. Tracy sat in the same spot as before and so did I. This time, the man that had piqued my interest walked up, leaned on his side of the bar, and asked if I was getting my usual.

The short, stocky guy took our orders and then my mystery man pointed to a flyer posted on the wall. The Jamaican Heritage Society was sponsoring a boat ride. Immediately I knew that I wanted to go, but before I could open my mouth, Tracy was already saying the wrong thing. "Girl, you better not get on that boat. You can't drink all of that water."

I was so embarrassed. I know I turned red. I closed my eyes and wished I could fly away.

When I finally opened my eyes and was able to look at my dark-chocolate crush, he smiled and asked me if I wanted to go. I was so shocked, all I could say was, "Huh?"

He said, "What about you? Would you like to come?" At this point, I felt defeated. There was no chance that I was going on a boat ride by myself. So that's what I told him. I felt a little embarrassed after saying it, but when I finally looked up, he said, "I'll go with you."

I looked over to Tracy to see if she heard him, but she was engrossed in a conversation of her own with one of the guys playing dominoes. My crush picked up one of the business cards from the front of the register and wrote his cell phone number on it. He told me to call him if I decided to come. That's when I found out his name: Errol Bellow. It sounded a little different, but it had a nice ring to it.

Other customers came in, so he was called away, but he cleared my plate and reminded me to call him about the tickets if I chose to go. I sat there for a few more minutes, waiting for Tracy to finish her conversation, and then we made our way to the car.

As we walked, she said, "Clarke, how long are you gonna come in here and buy chicken before you tell this man that you like him. This shit is getting crazy!"

I listened to her rant, and then I dropped the bomb. I couldn't hold back the laughter anymore. I handed her his card, and when she saw the handwritten number at the bottom, she said, "Damn, girl, I guess you do have your own way of doing things."

"The shortest skirt does not always win the man, Tracy."

The next week ran by as I rushed to get ready for the boat ride. Tracy finally agreed to go with me, and I was so excited. I couldn't wait to call Errol. I even took a day off work to get my hair and nails done.

Later that evening, we were boarding *The Eros* to begin a two-hour dance cruise down the Cape Fear River. Tracy and I spotted him—or I guess I should say *them*—first. He was standing with a group of about seven or eight other guys. Deanna's words came back to my mind, but I quickly swept them away. It was almost time to board when I got a call on my cell phone.

He had no idea that I was watching him. I could see the look of concern on his face as he scanned the crowd. I even saw the look of relief when he was able to pinpoint us amid the throngs of people as we spoke briefly on the phone. He didn't come over to greet me, and other than a few stolen glances, he didn't communicate with me again until we were on the boat.

Tracy and I found seats on the lowest of the three decks, but it gave us a decent view of all three. Once we'd gone a few minutes into the ride, Errol walked toward us with two dudes flanking him on both sides. It was in such a discreet manner that you could have missed it, but some things just don't get by me. He asked if we were having a good time, thanked us for coming, and moved on to greet an elderly couple sitting close by.

I saw the expression on Tracy's face. Words were not necessary; we'd been friends for a long time. We knew the game, so it was an unspoken decision from that point on just to make the best of the night.

We asked a young couple to hold our seats, and we were off to the bar. As we stood in line, I noticed the strobe light catching the pinwheel design on my dress. Suddenly I looked like a walking disco ball. Tracy and I could not hold back our laughter, but she knew this was fashion suicide, so she agreed to stay in line while I sat down.

I saw Errol and his brother approach her, and then she began to walk back toward her seat beside me. He asked her for our drink order and had his nephew bring us each a drink.

He came to our table again, and we thanked him for the drink. He asked me to save him a dance, and I said I would. But this was the last kindness of the evening. A few minutes later he was tearing the floor up with an older brown-skinned lady in a white dress.

Tracy and I were floored. She felt just as bad for me as I did for myself. Our story was the same: two country girls, stuck in time and looking for love in all the wrong places.

She said, "Damn, girl, that's fucked up. When this boat stops, we are going to be the first ones on the ground."

And that is exactly what we did. When the boat docked, we were out. We were almost back home when my phone rang. It was Errol asking where I was. I told him we'd left and I was almost home. He asked me to call him when I got there.

I was mad as hell, but all in all, this man had only sold me two fifty-dollar tickets. It was game. Errol Bellow was simply a very convincing salesman. It wasn't his fault that my feelings were hurt. It was mine. I assumed too much too quickly. It was definitely time to regroup. Maybe I'd just wait and let love find me. Anyway, it seemed that all the trouble came when I tried to chase it down.

Tracy dropped me off, and my phone was ringing as I stuck my key in the door. It was already after midnight, and Errol was offering to take me to a club that was two hours away. Clubs in Raleigh stayed open later, but he hadn't danced with me when he had the chance, and I wasn't going anywhere that late.

Hell, I knew what he was up to. It was too late and I was too tired to play the game, but Errol did not give up easily. He offered to take me to the local liquor house, a hole-in-the-wall night club that had almost weekly shootouts and stabbings, and finally, the Waffle House. I knew what he was selling, but I wasn't buying. He relented but agreed to call me later in the week.

A couple days passed, and finally the phone rang. Errol was calling with another invitation. This time it was an overnight trip to Myrtle Beach for some type of Jamaican celebration.

The beautiful thing about the invitation was his promise to get a separate room for me and a friend if I wanted. The messed-up part was none of my friends wanted to go. It didn't matter. I decided to go anyway.

For the next few nights we talked on the phone for hours. I felt like a high school kid again. I had something to look forward to when I got home from work. It broke the monotony of my boring-ass life.

The idea of love made me feel a hope that I thought was long gone, and I had high hopes.

On our day of departure, he was about an hour late picking me up. Once we made the hour-long drive to the beach, there was a rush to change our clothes. It was August 6, and we were going to party and celebrate Jamaica's Independence Day.

Club 843 was packed. It was still before eleven, and the parking lot was full already. Errol parked in front of the club in a small line of cars by the door. A familiar face from the restaurant opened the door for him. The two of them walked around the car to my side, and the guy just stood there as Errol opened the door for me. He held my hand as I got out of the car, and he introduced me to a dark-skinned guy named Kat. Kat was about five eleven and was built like a football player. He was wearing a button-up shirt, but you could tell he packed muscles underneath. I said a quick hello and switched my glance back to Errol.

He placed his hand on the small of my back and led me into the club. He found me a seat, brought me a waitress, and told me to order whatever I wanted.

Then he was approached by two guys from the restaurant. He bid me a quick good-bye and promised to be right back, but he was gone for almost an hour. During that time, there were two more guys from the restaurant seated at a table behind me.

I watched Errol as he weaved his way through the crowd, talking to various people while I sat at a table alone. It seemed that he couldn't get five or ten feet without someone wanting to shake his hand or have a conversation, but I also noticed that there was always someone to his left and right. I thought it may have been a coincidence at first, but I watched this pattern all night long.

When he moved, he was never alone. No big thing, right? When you go to the club with your girls, you stick together, but something seemed funny about the way things were going down. Something was going on.

I stopped my waitress to ask her where the ladies' room was, and when I got up to go, I noticed one of the guys sitting behind me get up too. When I came out of the bathroom and rounded the corner, he was standing there with a drink in his hand. I went back to my seat, and he went back to his.

As the music continued to play, I felt more comfortable and was finally able to enjoy myself. The Hennessey shots had given me a bit of liquid courage, and I was caught up in the off-beat sounds of the drums that were filling the air.

It was a more upscale place than I'd assumed it would be. It was packed, and the smell of marijuana filled the air. There were so many people, I couldn't tell where it was coming from. There was a bar in three of the four corners of the room. There was also a projection screen that showcased a slide show with pictures of the Jamaican flag, Jamaica's beautiful beaches and countryside, and later a live feed that chronicled the night's events.

It was easy to point out couples. Most of them were dressed alike, and there was no doubting they were together. How ironic that Errol and I were wearing complimentary outfits. He wore a white, linen pair of pants and suit jacket with a white T-shirt underneath. I was wearing a gold, green, and white ankle-length, tie-dye dress with gold heels. My hair was slicked back so it couldn't fall if I began to sweat. I had skipped the necklace and wore a pair of gold hoops—the big ones—and a big, gold bangle. We were a picture-perfect match.

When Errol returned, the crowd seemed to part and make way for us as he held my hand and led me to our table. The people that greeted him called him Elder, but it was too noisy at the time to ask him why. I would have to remember to ask about that later.

The dance floor was filled with women of every shape and color. Most were wearing short and shorter dresses. A lot of the women wore colored hair, but it was tasteful. It didn't seem as ghetto as it did back home.

I looked at these women wind on the dance floor and wondered what the hell Errol was doing with me. I was too stiff to move my hips like that. I had about three moves in my bag of tricks, and none of that was included. I imagined making my body move like that, but I didn't know whether to move my waist or my thighs. Then I tried to figure out which part to move first so I'd looked like them when they did it.

I wanted to try it, but this wasn't the place. Tonight was not the night to experiment. I knew I would probably stand out when I started my two-step, but it worked.

All the men were wearing some type of button-up shirt. All the ones with Errol were wearing blazers as well. People seemed to know and respect the group. It was as if everyone knew who they were. While we had direct access to the dance floor, our area was separated from the regular floor. We sat on a VIP platform of sorts. Two guys stood at the foot of the entrance to the section and turned people away when they tried to join us.

There were two tables on either side of us filled with guys from the Port City and a few other guys I didn't know. They didn't talk much, but I could tell they were important. There were too many people catering to them for them not to be. A couple of them were talking to women, but the rest were drinking and chatting it up. I listened as they laughed at some of the women on the dance floor.

A camera crew was circulating around the room, followed by a crew of two or three people taking photos. There was a real party going on there, and they were catching it all on tape. When the camera crew came in our direction, Kat asked the guy not to film our section. He seemed to be one of Errol's closest friends, and all of the other guys respected him.

The cameraman said, "I can film anywhere I want in this club."

Kat replied, "Look, man, I'll give you one more chance to leave."

The cameraman told the light operator to turn on the headlamp. But he quickly replied, "Man, I don't want any trouble." He set the headlamp on the floor by the stairs and quickly walked away. But the other asshole seemed determined to film us anyway.

Kat snatched the camera from the man's hand, threw it on the floor, and began to stomp on it. The cameraman started yelling, and security came rushing over and yelled at Kat, "Yo, man, what are you doing?"

But when he got within reach, he changed his tune and began to scold the cameraman. "Why are you bothering these nice people?"

"Hiram is the club owner here, not you," the cameraman said. "He told me I can film everyone and everything in this club. These people are no exception."

The security guard was well aware of who I was with, even though I wasn't. He whispered something to the angry cameraman, whose eyes got as big as fifty-cent pieces. The cameraman began bowing with his hands folded as if he were praying. He kept saying, "I'm sorry. I didn't know. Are we cool? I didn't know, man. Please forgive me."

Kat walked away, and the man saw that as his cue to leave with what was left of his camera and light fixtures while he could.

I went to the bathroom three more times that night, and the same guy followed me every time. Damn, Deanna was right. There was some funny shit going on.

Errol Bellow

I hated to leave Clarke alone, but I had to handle my business. She looked fabulous in that dress. It hugged her curves in a way that was seductive, but not sleazy. This separated her from three-quarters of the women in the club. She had class and a sense of pride some women never discover. Wearing her shoulders out was a great look, too. I'd been watching her a long time, and I wanted to make her feel as good as she looked. That would be my real reward for the evening. She would sleep with a king, and I, a queen.

In a small room off the side of the main office, I was forced back to reality, as I became surrounded by money. I set up this party so the Kings could come in undetected—even the hidden ones. Tickets were twenty dollars each, and there were over three thousand people there. The first three hours of the bar belonged to me too. Beautiful manicured hands had just given me sixty thousand dollars. It was a good night.

I wanted to get this meeting out of the way so I could celebrate my new position within the Kings with my lady. The Kings never brought their women into meetings, so I knew Clarke may be getting a little uneasy. I didn't know how she would adapt to the culture shock I was sure she was facing.

I removed the last twenty dollars from the money counter, placed the money in a large gym bag with a lock, and put it in a locked closet in the main office. One of the guys kept watch over the money while I made my way across the hall into the conference room, where a small crowd was gathering. I went inside, and my brother, Admiral, came into the room a few moments later.

He greeted everyone and made small talk as he went to the head of the table. He brought the group to attention as his gavel pounded the table. The gavel was small, but the sound echoed through the room. Everyone took a seat.

All five kings were there. Two of us would oversee the day-to-day operations; the other three were the hidden hands. They kept attorneys, cops, judges, and other public officials in our pocket, and we paid them a hefty price for their services. In return, they saw that all our planes flew, boats sailed, and—most importantly—that our cargo was never searched.

I didn't blame Admiral for taking his time to make the announcement. These were his last few moments as king. We were all labeled kings, but there was only one leader. Admiral had done well for himself and the council, but now he spent too much time in the islands to handle the East Coast market properly. Today he would hand it over to me. This is what the party was for; they were there to celebrate my elevation in the family.

I was glad that Clarke was there to share the evening with me, despite the fact that she didn't know what she was celebrating. I wasn't sure about letting her know the full scope of my business partnerships. I wasn't thinking of the beauty of the moment, nor did I try to savor it. My thoughts were of Clarke.

The room quieted as Admiral began to speak. He thanked everyone for their loyalty to such a profitable organization and told us he would be retiring in Jamaica and would work from there.

The transition was a simple one. He called me to the head of the table, hugged my neck, shook my hand, and placed his ring on my finger. The act was done. The room was full of applause, and I was now the top of the food chain.

I decide what packages went where and who moved them. Those decisions were the easy ones. The more difficult ones were deciding when someone would live or die. My heart was big, which made my job hard. I've cried at night over the men I've had to murder. I've cried for the wives and children that would miss them, but this business allowed for no mercy. Being nice could get you killed.

I remembered this as the five men in the room greeted me and wished me well. They loved me because we'd been through the struggle together, but each secretly wanted to be next in line or envied me for having the seat in the first place. Biggie had it right: "more money, more problems."

The door opened, and waitresses came in with bottles of champagne. We each had our own as we toasted to our future. I was no longer the barefoot boy from the red hills of Jamaica. I was a *boss*—the big man in the white suit.

The Clock Struck Midnight

I was a little uneasy sitting there in the VIP with Errol's crew, but it felt good to be with them. I had no idea what was going on around me, but it was nice to be catered to, and I was caught in the trance of the night. The bass had the floor shaking, and I think I had a contact. The air reeked of marijuana, and everyone was of one spirit. These people were really celebrating, and it felt good to be in the number.

I don't know how many times I stopped the waitress, but I know I'd drunk a lot, because I really had to pee again. I felt the effects of the alcohol as soon as I stood up. I was a little unsteady as I made my way around the corner to the ladies' room.

I was only about ten steps outside of the VIP area when I felt someone's hand on my shoulder. I turned around, and this guy was smiling at me with a mouth full of gold teeth. It was the funniest thing I'd seen all night. His tiny dreadlocks looked like small snakes sticking out all over his head. He had on a gold chain with a Jesus piece on it almost as big as the palm of my hand.

He said, "I wondered when you were gonna come down off that throne so I could holla at you."

"I am with someone, I'm sorry."

It didn't take him a split second to respond. "He's not with you now, is he?"

Just then one of the guys from the restaurant tapped the guy on the shoulder and whispered something into his ear. He didn't seem to be a willing participant as two guys herded him into the men's bathroom. A third told me to go on into the ladies' room. That was the last hiccup of the evening. When I returned to the table, Errol was back.

Pretty soon I was rocking and reeling to sounds that I'd never heard before, yet felt so familiar. I felt a hand on my waist and the mold of a man behind me. It was funny, though; he didn't touch me in a way that was at all intrusive or offensive. It was reassuring and confident. I leaned back on his chest, and we just swayed to the beat for a while.

The evening was perfect as a reggae version of Marvin Gaye's "Let's Get It On" filled the air. I loved the sense of protection I felt in Errol's strong arms. Other couples were daggering. That was definitely something new. These guys were picking up ladies twice my size and bouncing them up and down on their laps as if they were light as a feather.

The ladies seemed to be enjoying it as their thongs were showing and their asses were out, but I was so glad that he didn't try to do that to me. I got that it was a part of their culture, but it definitely wasn't for me. Another song began to play and Errol left me to join the group of guys.

I watched Errol, Kat, Admiral, and the rest of their buddies jump around to the music. It almost seemed animal-like, the way they threw their legs and arms around. I was a deer in headlights, a new person in a strange land, and I loved it.

The music slowed down even more, and Morgan Heritage's "She's Still Loving Me" was playing. Errol left the group of guys he was surrounded with and grabbed my hand.

He pulled me to the center of our area. And suddenly the spotlight was on us. We were literally on the dance floor, and the spotlight had shifted to us as the Port City crew circled us like a hedge. They all stood with crossed arms and smiling faces.

These guys were on top of the world, and at that exact moment I was too. There was no denying the feelings that were stirring between Errol and me. I was pissed after being ignored on the boat ride, but this more than made up for it. I preferred this atmosphere to that one, anyway.

Once the song was over, we both felt it was time to call it a night. Something magical had just happened.

He steered me to the exit, again with his hand on the small of my back. There were two guys from the restaurant in front of us and two behind. The car had been pulled to the entrance, and the motor was running. This man really knew how to roll out the red carpet.

Our drive back to the hotel was filled with questions about the music and the culture. I was fascinated, and Errol smiled as I bombarded him. This was my first up-close experience with another culture. Tonight had been different from anything I'd ever experienced or expected. The girls would never believe it.

He opened the door and wrapped his arms around me as we walked into the hotel. It was so innocent. I felt like I was being courted. It felt good. The effects of the alcohol were kicking in more as he helped me to balance myself on the cobblestone walkway that led to the entrance of the hotel. He tried to steady me, but it seemed that it only moved me further from achieving balance. Finally I just had to lean on him. Otherwise I would have fallen on my face.

I lay across the bed after taking off my shoes, and I must have dozed off, because I woke up as his fingers moved across my back. It was the best feeling I'd had in a long time.

I closed my eyes to enjoy it. His hands moved slowly but methodically across the part of my back exposed by my tube top dress. Every muscle that he massaged was connected to a nerve ending in my underwear. He was rubbing my back, but everything below my waist was hot and throbbing.

I think he noticed as I began to squirm under his hands. I couldn't turn over to see, though. Turning over would be admitting that I liked it or that I wanted to take it to the next step, and I didn't want to do that, so I pretended to be asleep. I let my head sink further into the pillow to add to the effect, but his hands never stopped moving.

I must have really dozed off, because I felt him lightly shaking me.

"Are you ready for bed now, sleepy head?" he said softly in that strong accent I was growing to love.

"Yes, I just need to take a shower." I tried to sound exhausted.

His face had the biggest grin, and I saw most of his teeth as he said, "Cool."

He began to take off his shirt. What in the world was happening? "Hey, hey," was all I could manage to say at first. Then I followed with "Alone!"

All the air was gone from his sails. I could see it. He didn't try to force himself on me. I was thankful for that, but did he really think I was going to shower with him? I hadn't even gotten used to my own weight-loss yet. I wasn't ready for him to see my body and definitely not in the shower together. I excused myself. I needed to get away from this man before my clothes started to come off.

I took a long shower, hoping he would fall asleep by the time I got out. My head was telling my body to calm down. This wasn't the right thing to do. But as I applied lotion to my legs and thighs, the other half of me didn't seem to agree.

It had been so long since I'd been filled down there, but I couldn't let it happen on the first night. How would that look? I would be the same as every other woman who came into that restaurant. Maybe I'd be lucky and he'd be asleep.

I emerged in a pair of green cheerleading shorts and a yellow and green turtle T-shirt smelling like Shea Butter and vanilla. Damn, I smelled good.

The room had double beds, and he'd already claimed one. I quickly got in the other.

Errol asked, "Why are you sleeping over there?"

"It's the right thing to do," I quickly responded.

He said, "If you're thinking that I will sleep with you and not call you again, you're wrong."

What? Was this nigga playing with my mind? He could have been with any woman in that club. Why was he choosing me? Had he really taken something away from those hours we'd spent on the phone before our trip?

Something in those big, beautiful, brown eyes reassured me that he meant what he said. There was hurt behind those eyes, but I wouldn't hurt him. I would love him, and he would let me.

I crossed the room to his bed. He held the covers back and slid over to make room for me.

I didn't know what to expect from this man. For a few seconds, I lay there with my eyes closed. I opened them to find him smiling at me.

"A penny for your thoughts?" he asked.

"I am not sure what you want with me, Errol."

"Clarke, I want to be with you. I want to feel you and feel for you. I know you think I will leave you, but I won't. I just need someone to be there for me when the lights go out."

I snapped, "And I want someone to be there for me when they come back on."

He laughed—the kind that comes from your gut and fills a room. "You have no idea how long I've admired you, do you?" he said.

"Admired me? What are you talking about?" I replied with a puzzled look on my face.

"Don't you remember me from the bank in Jacksonville? I used to come in and make the Marley Grill deposit every Tuesday."

Oh my goodness. I did remember. It was him. When I worked at the bank, my coworker Tiffany used to go on and on about him. This was too bad for her. She wanted him; I got him. Now I just had to hook him.

"Errol, I do remember you. My coworker Tiffany loved you. She wanted you so badly. I don't know if we should be together."

"That's not my problem, Clarke, and it's not yours. That is her problem. I always wanted you. Can you say that I ever accepted her advances?"

"No."

"That's because I had no intentions for her. But let me be clear about the ones I have for you." He leaned in and kissed me.

I liked it and didn't stop him as his kisses moved from my mouth to the nape of neck. My body was turned up. I felt the juices as they began to flow. I wished they would stop. How could my mouth say no when my body was responding so differently?

In one motion, he'd removed my shirt and had one of my nipples in his mouth as he turned the other with his hand. If this man didn't stop now, I wouldn't be able to stop him later. The truth was, I didn't want to, and I didn't.

He kissed my body all over and I allowed it. I didn't even try to touch him back, but I could tell that he didn't need much motivation. The proof was already poking me in my leg.

Our first time was magical. He took his time and discovered hidden spots that delivered sensations that I didn't know were possible. But I didn't feel cheapened by the experience.

This man was really making me feel good. I didn't have to fake it or do it myself. He had it all covered. He massaged my insides in a way that said, "I am here." He slowly explored my corners and depths with a wind of his own. I was only too happy to keep up with it.

I came twice before he even tried to get one for himself. He was already different than my usual. I got mine. For the first time in a long time, I got me. The tears ran down my face as he kissed them away and slowed his stroke. This man could read my mind. His dick was stroking my walls and my ego.

He slowed his stroke even more and said, "Clarke, this is it for me. I have wanted you for a long time. Now I have you. There is no need to let go or be afraid. I won't hurt you."

This time as he kissed me, he climaxed. As my hips began to roll, I could feel him throbbing as he let out a moan so loud that I needed to put my hand over his mouth. For a second, he had the look of a scolded schoolboy, but he removed my hand, leaned down, and began to kiss me even deeper than before.

Then we just lay there, still connected, with his head on my chest. I am not sure when we fell asleep or when he slipped out, but when I woke up the next morning, I was still in his arms. And after wishing me a good morning, he did it all over again.

I was hooked, but what I didn't know was that he was too.

We showered, grabbed some breakfast at the local IHOP, and enjoyed our ride back to reality. We laughed and really enjoyed each other's company on our way home. After an hour, I had an idea of what it was like to grow up poor in Jamaica, and he understood what it was like to grow up in rural North Carolina. Suddenly he didn't seem so intriguing. He was a country boy who wanted to create a better life for his family. He and I really weren't so different.

I am not sure when I dozed off, but when I woke up, we were in front of my house and he was needed at the restaurant.

The fairy-tale evening was over. I was back to real life.

A Reason for it All

That night was the best night of my life. It wasn't only because I was tapped the new Don Datta; I was finally happy. Women were a dime a dozen and always trying to get in my face, but I finally found the one who wasn't about all the bullshit. Business was booming and life was good, but it was different this time. I was always gonna make money, but I had a different use for it now. I wanted to enjoy it with the family I've always wanted.

I'd finally connected with the love of my life, even though she never noticed I was looking. Clarke hadn't remembered me, but I sure remember seeing her at Fort City National Bank every Tuesday, but we were in Jacksonville then. I had no idea the bank was based in the Port City or that I'd ever see her again.

I don't know why I liked her so much back then. I think it's because she was different. My brothers and I were pretty well known in Jacksonville, especially at the bank. We made pretty sizeable deposits into the

Marley Grill account. It was hard to get out of the bank without some teller or customer asking for my number, mentioning how loaded I was, or asking if I was married.

I hated it. I could walk in the door and captivate anyone's attention—except hers. Tiffany, from the bank, always seemed to want me at her station. Time and time again, she would find some reason to kill time when serving a customer so I could be her next patron. Last Tuesday, she recounted her money drawer. She got up for a drink of water two weeks ago and got up to make a phone call the week before that. Tuesday I would beat her at her own game. I wanted to speak to Clarke. I had to see what she was about. This was important for me.

My deposit was just over eight thousand dollars. It was usually around five or six thousand, but this time I added a couple thousand. Tiffany's station was free, and she smiled at me as I opened the door. I held the door for an elderly gentleman behind me and went to the island to pretend to fill a deposit slip. Scott always filled out the deposit slips before I left the restaurant, but I needed to buy some time. The gentleman walked right past me to Tiffany's station, so I made my way to my real destination.

Her head was down as I approached her. She was turning all the faces of her money the same way. I thought I was the only one who did that. This woman was amazing. I loved her respect for money and instantly wanted to know more about her. She clipped the bills together and called, "Next." She did all of this before she ever looked up, but when she did, I had a seat in front of her.

"Good morning, how may I help you?"

"Yes, I'd like to make a deposit."

Then I handed her our deposit. She didn't gasp or go on about it like the other young ladies there. She threw the twenties on her counter and paper clipped them into five-hundred-dollar bundles. Then she wrapped them in two-thousand-dollar bands. She didn't fumble like Tiffany as she tried to hand count my money and smile in my face at the same time. Hell, last time we had to recount it. Scott was never wrong. Clarke hand counted the fives and ones with such precision that it turned me on. She had the same respect for money that I did. I was amazed.

When she finally spoke, she said, "You are my new favorite customer."

Damn, she was the same as the rest of these money-hungry options in there, but I humored her and asked, "Why do you say that?"

"Because you turn all your faces the same way. You saved me a lot of time." All I could do was laugh. That wasn't the answer I'd expected.

I said, "I'm picky about that too."

"Here is your receipt, Mr. Bellow. Is there anything else I can help you with?"

"Lunch."

"Excuse me?" Again, this isn't the answer I was looking for.

"I'm sorry; I assumed you knew me too."

"No. Is there a reason I should know you?"

"I own the Marley Grill on Madison Street. You should come by and try some of our Jamaican cuisine" was all I could think to say.

"That's not really my thing, but if I ever get a wild hair, I'll come through."

The next time I went to the bank, she was gone. Damn, you win some, you lose some. I didn't pretend to smile at Tiffany, and from then on Scott made the deposits. Clarke had quit to work somewhere else, and I didn't see her again until she walked into my restaurant four years later.

There is no way to describe my shock as I saw her walk into the restaurant to pick up her order. This was the lady from the bank—in my restaurant. I remember Kat and the rest of the guys in the kitchen noticed my demeanor change as we watched the door from behind the two-way glass wall that covered the back of the restaurant. Kat leaned in and asked, "Is everything all right, boss?"

"Kat, I think she is the one. She found me." I patted him on the shoulder so he would get out of my way. I was ringing up this order. She was very polite as she handed me a crisp twenty-dollar bill. She thanked me and was out of the door.

After all those years, I had missed the opportunity again. By this time, the cousins came out from the back with Kat and began to talk smack to me. "Errol is love struck," Kat said. "Out of all those women that come in here day after day, what makes you want that one? She is country and plain."

"Kat, that's why I like her. What are we, if not country and plain? We hide behind gold watches and designers clothes, but we all came from the same shack on the same dirt road. Don't forget it, dude. That is what makes us who we are. That is what makes us the Kings." I played that day over in my head as the restaurant door opened.

Playtime was over, and it was back to business as Mike walked in to make his drop. He'd been having a problem with a couple of his guys. They wanted larger percentages from him. And to be honest, he could have paid it, but he was just too stingy. He was the lieutenant of his team, and those decisions were left up to him—until they impacted my cut, and that's what had happened.

This ass clown let two members of his team get fronts they never paid for, and in turn, he couldn't pay me. This was a problem. I liked Mike. He was a hard-working fast talker that made me lots of money. I explained early on that when he didn't make me lots of money, he should disappear or find another occupation. I hoped that today wasn't the day to make that decision.

I was an elder in the game around there. I was the one people came to when their folks were out of order. I was the peacemaker or the rainmaker. The Kings placed that decision on my head. I liked Mike, but it was time for action.

A few of his drops were short last year, but that was around the time Dee lost the twins. I knew he needed to get her away for a while, and I gave him a three-month pass to catch up. He did, and we never had another issue. The fact that we hung out once a week as Scott counted my money didn't make us friends, and he had obviously gotten that twisted.

Mike walked in with his normal walk. It made all my cousins laugh. It looked like someone shot him in one of his legs, but he thought it was cool. The ladies may have loved it, but it always made him appear to be trying too hard. Today my intuitions rang out a little too loudly for me.

My brother, Admiral, my ace, was always skeptical of him. He said he was too eager. I thought a little ambition was a great thing. He advised me to show no mercy in my dealing with Mike. He never trusted him and had been waiting to drop the hammer on him for years.

I sat at the last table near the kitchen door of the restaurant. This kept me close to the kitchen and allowed a hidden king to watch from behind the double-sided glass that made up our back wall. This way, all action was sanctioned.

Mike came in and sat at my table. Kat and Black were behind me. Scott was sitting by the bar with two cousins, and the usual gang was seated by the domino table. Only this time there was no laughing and joking. All eyes were on Mike.

As he sat across from me he said, "What's up, man?"

"Mike," I said, "do you really come in here and speak to me as if we are friends when your bag is light? That is certainly not how you treat a friend."

"I know, I know, Errol. It's just been hard out here lately. These young guys have it in their head that they don't have to pay me. I've gone to their moms, their baby moms. Hell, I even checked the side chicks' houses and can't find these niggas."

"Mike, you misunderstand the situation, my stupid friend."

He did not like being called stupid. I could tell by the way he sat up in his chair when I said it. I knew he was getting heated, but he knew what would happen if he acted up.

I went on. "Anything that happens to my product after you receive it is of no consequence to me. You will pay me and you will do it in forty-eight hours. You have my permission to take two cousins with you to handle this. You will pay me. You will pay them half of your profit and you do with rest as the streets allow."

"Now, please understand that we are not friends and you will find yourself in the rain if you are short again. No excuses and no exceptions."

"Thank you, Errol. You won't be sorry, I promise," Mike pleaded as he stood up to make his way to the door.

Black stopped him as he got away to leave. "Empty your pockets, Mike."

"What?"

"Errol, call off your dude, man?"

"Mike, you forget—we are not friends. Don't worry, man. We'll take it off your bill."

He had a couple thousand in his pocket. I split it up between the guys in the restaurant after Mike sat at our calculator and figured out what the cut for twelve people would be.

He was not very happy as he left me that day, but I chose to attack his pride and spare his life. I only hoped he appreciated the gesture. If he didn't, the streets would tell me, and it would rain anyway.

Mike had a chalk line to walk. He wanted this life. We would see if he measured up to the lifestyle he portrayed. I felt better with cousins there to watch him. The family would always look out for the best interests of the family. They would make sure he held up his end of the deal.

As soon as he was gone, my mind switched back to the beautiful young lady who was stealing my heart.

Mike Daybrahm

I didn't understand how all these niggas out there could make more money than me. I knew Dee was gonna kill me when I get home and couldn't pay the rent. She was on me pretty bad about my lifestyle and how I didn't need it if it didn't at least pay the bills. She said I was absorbing the risk for someone else, and she was right, but that was the only way to come up in the business. It didn't matter how much money you had; it mattered what kind of connect you have.

And I had the connect. In the beginning, this other Jamaican dude was supplying my man Kat, and I was doing such numbers with him that he turned me on to his boss. The process wasn't fast or easy. These were some strange motherfuckers. One night, Kat called after two and told me to come take a ride. He took me to the country—where exactly, I couldn't tell you—but we pulled up to a group of storage units in the middle of nowhere. Kat typed in a code, and we drove in.

He didn't drive straight to the unit. He drove around it a couple of times, but I didn't say anything. I just took the ride. When Kat finally stopped, he knocked on a storage unit door. But it wasn't the usual knock, knock, knock. It was something he was doing on purpose. Then there was a knock from the other side of the door. Kat didn't knock anymore, and then we just stood there.

Then the door came up. At first it looked just like any other storage building; it even had boxes and power tools lining the wall. I began to feel a little uneasy. Why did this clown get me outta my bed to come to a fucking storage building? I was opening my mouth to say that when Kat said, "Hey, Mike, follow me, man. It's just around these boxes."

As we turned the corner, I saw a door cut into the wall of the storage unit. Kat pushed a doorbell, and the door opened. I couldn't believe this shit. It looks like they had connected four or five units and built a conference room of sorts. The inside wasn't as wide as I expected. In fact, it was kinda narrow, but it was a great place to hide some shit.

That dude from the restaurant named Errol was sitting in a corner, having a drink with some other guy. They had to be brothers or at least first cousins. They didn't exactly look alike, but you knew they were close kin. There were two men standing on both sides of them, wearing holsters with guns in them. This nigga named Lee, from around the way, was seated at another table across the room. I knew him. I didn't fuck with him though. Something about him never sat well with me. He talked too much, and I kept my distance from him in the streets.

Kat took me to the table with Lee. I was immediately pissed, but this didn't seem like the time to complain. He pulled up a chair and sat there with us. He and Lee made small talk.

Suddenly Errol and this other guy walked up to the table. They sat at the two chairs on the opposite side of the table. Errol was the first to speak. "Both of you guys are here for the same reason. You are here because we help you make money. We allow you to be here and to live well out there because you do the same for us. You are here to make us money. This means when you get a front from me and you don't pay—you pay. We hope you understand this concept. Do you understand this concept?"

Oh, shit. I just realized this nigga was waiting for an answer. "Yeah, I get it. Everybody eats."

"Okay, Mike," Errol said. "I see that you get the concept. Kat has vouched that you understand it, but I want you to understand that Kat vouched for the nigga sitting beside you too."

Errol looked at Lee and said, "Is there any reason this agreement shouldn't work out for all of us?"

"No," he replied and put his head down.

"Then where the fuck is my money?" Errol screamed.

"Well, Errol, it's—"

"No, nigga, let me make this simple: Today is your deadline. Do you have my money?"

As soon as Lee got the word *no* out of his mouth, a bullet pierced his head. Oh, shit. I had just watched this nigga take his last breath.

Errol told me to go stand against the wall and motioned for me to go to the other side of the dimly lit room. I saw this nigga get shot, but I didn't know where the bullet came from. I didn't know what the fuck was going on, but I knew how to follow directions. These niggas obviously didn't play.

Kat picked up the card table that was just in front of me and threw it into a small, metal container inside the unit. I hadn't seen it before, but we were sitting on a big square of plastic on top of an area rug. He laid Lee's limp body out on the plastic and began to roll it up. Once he'd rolled and taped Lee up in the rug, he took off his gloves and threw them into the metal bin along with Lee and the chairs.

Then he asked me to join him in the corner with Errol and the other dude. Errol said, "So, are you sure that you want to make even more money for me? It seems we have a vacancy."

"Yeah, man. It's out there and I wanna get it." I put my hands in my pocket so they wouldn't see them shaking.

"Everyone wants to get it," Errol said. "And they may, but do you have what it takes to keep it? Our organization is about secrecy. This is what ensures longevity. Can you keep a secret, Mike?"

"Ask your man Kat about me. He hasn't kept me around for nothing. I've made about a hundred thousand for you in the last five months. That seems like a pretty good reason to keep me around."

"That's what Lee thought too. Look, I didn't come to count the cow; I came for its milk. So here is the deal: your numbers go up, but so does your tax. You get it for less than anywhere else, so if you have any questions, get out. Otherwise, let's get this money."

"Aight, Errol, I'm down. Let's get this money."

"Hey, Mike, if you ever decide that you want to stop breathing, be short, okay?"

I nodded and managed to say, "Not a problem for me; I can count."

This was all before that white girl took over everything. Everyone is running around yelling, "Once you go black, you never go back," but they never met that white girl. I sold this shit and I knew her power, but I never thought I would use it.

Covering it up wasn't a problem for me at first. It was just something I did with the fellas to stay awake on those longs nights while moving packages along those country roads. As the runs increased, so did my intake. As time passed, it became just like a friend to me. If I was having a bad day, she was there. If Dee was nagging me, she was there.

And everything was fine until I lost count and pulled from the street supply. I'd done it once or twice before, but I'd never used this much. I was still moving packages in the street and everything was coming in on time; I just used more than I could afford to put back.

Dee was beginning to notice that something was wrong. I hadn't helped her with the major bills in over three months, and she was getting fed up. She didn't deserve this shit, and I knew it. I knew how much she loved me. It's just that when those feelings of anger or fear or desperation came, I needed it.

Dee's love for me was powerful, but I didn't trust it to get me through. I just needed to clear my head and get this nigga his money before people began to look for me the same way they've been looking for Lee for the last three years. I didn't have my rent, but I had my life. I'd seen Errol have niggas murked for way less than ten thousand dollars.

Dee

I moved to the Port City to go to college. I didn't know anyone in the city, so I decided to spend my time volunteering. I had to borrow my roommate's car and draw a map to get to the Port City Community Boys and Girls Club. During the course of things at the club, I'd lost my map. Another student volunteer tried to give me directions, and I thought I had them down until I found myself on Market Street.

I was driving really slow and looking for familiar street signs, when I looked up at a nice chocolate drop driving an Acura Vigor. I immediately pulled into the Wendy's parking lot and felt my pride grow as he pulled in behind me. By the time we pulled in, cars were beginning to pull in behind us. The handsome man in the Acura told me to drive across the street, and that was the first of many times that I took direction from Mike.

He was in a hurry and didn't have a lot of time. In less than five minutes, he knew I attended the local university and had my phone number and the name of my dorm. I had something to look forward to for the first time since I'd gotten there. He said he'd be tied up for the next couple of days, but he'd give me a call.

Mike didn't call until two days later. That was worse than him not asking for the number at all. By that time, I was so aggravated that I really didn't want to be bothered. I had spent the last two days on pins and needles every time the phone would ring. The dorm phone didn't have caller ID, so every ring of the phone made my heart race and my palms sweaty.

After two days of that, I was exhausted. The phone rang and my roommate said, "Dee, it's for you." The voice on the other end of the phone told me he was downstairs and asked me to come down to talk. I was in a pair of gray Spandex pants with a T-shirt and slides. I was hardly ready for a meet and greet. I explained my dilemma, but Mike didn't care.

I brushed back my ponytail and ran to catch the elevator. I walked out of the building, and this fine-ass man was sitting on the bench outside the dorm. He flashed a pearly white smile I will never forget while wearing a bright-orange shirt and white Air Force Ones. I had to check out his shoes, because my grandfather always taught his girls that a man will treat you no better than he does his shoe. His shoes were brand-new, bright white with immaculate laces.

Our first hug was so awkward I wished it never happened. It seemed I had too many arms, and one managed to hit him in the face. He was stunned, but recovered well. "I know not to mess with you."

"Yep, I am a country girl, and I used to fight my boy cousins for fun. Don't try me." We both laughed, and suddenly I didn't feel so awkward.

Our conversation lasted for about an hour. It turned out that he was from South Carolina and knew as much about picking and shelling peas, and cow tipping as I did. It was a relief to meet someone who was relatable. After I felt comfortable enough around him, I asked him why it took so long to call.

He told me he was tied up. I said, "I'm gonna leave that alone, but if you were with a lady, you can just leave."

He laughed at me and asked me to take a ride with him. I was happy enough to take him up on that offer. He began to drive around the city. He explained the roads in a way that made sense. I was finally learning my city.

Then we started to go to places I'd never seen before. The buildings weren't as nice and did not look as friendly as other areas of town. Townhouses with porches, columns, and fancy roofs were replaced with cinderblock buildings painted gray. They looked a bit scary to me at first, but I think they were just sad.

Mike would drive to these neighborhoods, pull into one of the parking lots, and tell me he'd be right back. I locked the door and waited. After the fourth or fifth parking lot, I was beginning to wonder what was really going on. He kept jumping out of the car, but he never came back with anything I could see.

I rode around with Mike for hours. Finally around ten, he dropped me off at my dorm so I could finish up some homework. He promised to pick me up at 11:30. He was ringing the phone at exactly 11:30, but it was to tell me that he was on his way. That was fine with me. I was just finishing my hair.

My stretch pants were now replaced with a pair of jeans, a Tommy Hilfiger polo, and a pair of boots. I was looking a little different this time. Mike must have been pleasantly surprised; he just kept smiling.

"You clean up well, don't you?"

"Whatever, dude. You didn't stop in the middle of Market Street for a mud duck, now, did you?"

We joked around until we got to our next destination. He described this place as a place that he and his homies went with their old ladies to chill. I had an immediate smile on my face. Did that mean he thought I was old lady material? I had to force myself to stop thinking. This was our first day together. I couldn't go planning the future already.

We went into a second-story apartment. He knocked on the door, and when it opened, I heard screaming and laughing.

"Mike finally got an old lady!"

"Hey, man," said the man behind the door. "I guess old Mike finally found someone to put up with his ass. Come on in." He shook my hand and dapped Mike up. Then I was introduced to the other men sitting at the bar. I met Kat, Black, and this other dude named Errol that night.

Then I was ushered into another room with a card table, big screen, couch, and tons of toys. There were two other ladies already seated. They introduced themselves: Clarke and Tracy.

Clarke was quick to ask me who I came with. She came off as very territorial. She had an attitude and a gap.

I ignored her issue and told her I was there with Mike. She busted out laughing and asked me if I wanted to be dealt in their game of Tunk.

Tracy said, "Don't let Clarke punk you. Her bark is worse than her bite."

"Yeah, unless I bite your ass." Clarke talked shit, but she seemed cool as a fan by the end of the evening.

About an hour later, Kat knocked on the door and was followed by the guys that greeted me at the door, each taking their woman to a spot on the sectional that covered the room. Then some guy named Lil Stupid ran in, yelling, "I just found this shit, man. It is the bomb. Have you seen it yet?"

He was talking about the movie *Belly* with Nas and DMX. I had heard of it but never seen it. I was amped. Mike brought me a drink, and we cuddled up on the couch like everyone else. I had just met all these people, and strangely enough, it felt like I was becoming a part of something. I felt like I was joining a family.

Belly was followed by *Shottas,* a movie about some Jamaican gangsters who grew up robbing and stealing. I was amazed. I was from a small town with two stoplights, and most of this was unfamiliar to me. Every small town has someone who sells a little crack and weed, but I didn't know that people did it like they did on those movies.

Then I made the mistake of saying it out loud. Kat said, "Don't you know who you are with?"

I said, "Yeah, I am with Mike." Laughter filled the room, and Mike said we had to go.

"Mike," I asked, "what was that guy talking about. Who am I with?"

He leaned in and kissed me, but he never answered the question.

As time passed, the answer became resoundingly clear.

Don't Go Back to That Apartment

That Woodly Brooke apartment quickly became our hangout spot. I started to look forward to hanging out with Dee and the crew once a week. It had been our routine for about a year, and I loved this family of ours.

Errol and I picked up a couple bottles of Moscato for the ladies and a few bottles of Hennessy for the guys, and we were off to the spot.

But when we walked in, the room was different. We didn't hear the chants of everyone saying hello. It was quiet as church in there. Errol kissed me on my forehead and told me to go say hi to Dee and Tracy, so I was on my way. I kept walking, but my ears were turned all the way up.

I heard Mike say, "Man, I can't help it. She just be talking too much. She don't know when to shut up."

At this point, I didn't even want to know what they were talking about. When I got to the room, it was kinda dark in there. I wasn't sure what was going on. Dee was sitting there by the light of the television, wearing a big pair of shades. Tracy was on the sectional, but she was obviously pissed.

"Dee," I asked, "are you okay?"

She opened her mouth but had no words. The tears began to stream down her face, and she took off her glasses. Then I saw it. Mike needed his ass kicked.

Dee had scratches all over her face. They weren't the small kind that babies leave when they scratch you or even the kind that your pet leaves when it scratches you. This scratch ran from one eye to another, across the bridge of her nose, but it wasn't the kind you see on a person. It looked like a carving.

I screamed, "Who did this to you?"

She began begging me to be quiet. I was so hype, I was shaking. I saw that I was only upsetting her more, so I sat down to hear her story. It turns out she and Mike had an argument. Dee had been visiting family and sent Mike 560 dollars to make her car note. But when she got back to town, he was nowhere to be found. She checked his pager and heard his sister warning him that Dee was back and that he'd better get home now.

I said, "Girl, what did you do?"

She said, "I went to his baby momma's house and found my truck hidden in a parking lot across the street. I keyed the car and went home and bleached his clothes."

For some reason, we both started to laugh. The pain was so real, we had to laugh to take its power. She went on with her story. "Mike was hiding the car because he never made the payment, so I put all the clothes that I just bought him with my Dad's Dillard's card in the tub and wrote the word *whore* on every pair of jeans I could find.

"Do you know how stupid I felt? My whole family warned me about this dude, but there is something about him that won't let me leave him alone. I wanted to find love for myself. Now he has proven them right, and I am too afraid to go to them. I just don't want to hear I told you so. And he begged me to stay, anyway."

"Girl, he even gave me a bath and bought me that new pair of 250-dollar sunglasses I'd been wanting," she said as she tried to muster up a laugh.

"Dee, that's not funny!"

"I know, girl, but let me laugh at it, okay? He promised me he won't do it again. He cried and snotted and even got on his knees. Maybe this will be what it takes to get us back on track. We just can't seem to get it right lately. He stays out until four or five in the morning and leaves around six or seven in the evening. He never has any money, and I think he owes Errol money too."

"I heard him explaining that some young cat named Rick had not paid him for some work he'd done, and that's why he was late paying Errol back."

I couldn't take it anymore. I had to ask.

"Dee, what do Errol and these guys do? Errol is always so secretive, and there are certain days in every week that he's busy. It is a woman or some bullshit. Which is it, Dee?"

Dee said, "Clarke—Errol is—"

The door swung open. It was Errol. He said, "Dee, he did this to you?"

Dee said, "You know how it goes. He just had a temper last night. I know it won't happen again."

"It better not. For now he gets half, and if he lays his hand on you again, I cut him off. We don't deal with that kind of man. You shouldn't either. Do you understand?"

I watched the tears start to stream down her face over layers of Neosporin, and she forced herself to say the word. "Yes."

Errol said, "We have to go." I hugged Dee and gave her my number to put in her phone. She had a new one; Mike broke the other one.

I said, "Dee, don't forget where we were. I want to start there when we talk again."

All for Love

I had nothing to say as Errol held Clarke's coat while she put her arms in it. He was so affectionate. He loved that woman. You could see it. Something about him was there to protect her. You could feel it.

I was torn. What do I say and what don't I say?

Clarke would never believe she was dating one of the Kings of the city. She thought she had a working man.

She was naive as hell, walking around like some princess with her head up in the sky. I didn't know if I wanted to ruin that for her. She needed to find it out on her own, like I did.

Things started out so well with Mike. It seemed like just moments since we met on Market Street, and I have no idea how we got to where we were. It seemed that he could never keep product. He stayed out all night and wanted to sleep all day. He didn't even take me back to campus for class anymore. He just gave me the car because he was so exhausted when he got home.

I wouldn't have cared if he came home with money, but it was always just enough to get groceries or pay one of his bills. Other than that, he was of no use to me. Something was going on. I wondered what had happened to my Mike.

The guys were really raggin' on Mike for the way he treated me. I knew that Errol cutting his supply this week wouldn't help things at home, but I was glad that someone was standing up for me. They made him stay to clean up.

I went outside to grab a cigarette out of the car and noticed one of the guys he picks up money from in the projects talking to someone in a black car and pointing toward the apartment. I was walking as if I hadn't seen them. I calmly walked back up the stairs and told Mike.

Suddenly he ran to the cabinet and pulled out a bag of onions. He began pulling back the skin on the whole pack. Then he asked me to call Kat and Black to come back. When they did, suddenly the apartment was filled with the smell of onions. Mike would pull the skin back; Kat would cut out a chunk; Black would put something in it, replug the hole, and pull the skin back.

They did this for an hour and even sent Lil Stupid out to get more onions. I don't know why he let them call him that. At times he was the smartest person in the room, but he never gave them any flack about it.

After the last onion was filled, they cleaned the house. I mean with Clorox, in gloved hands. Lil Stupid vacuumed the floor. Kat made a call. I heard him say Errol's name, but when he saw me looking at him, he went into another room. Then he came back and told us it was okay to leave. He pulled Mike, Black, and Lil Stupid in a room, and then they all left but Mike.

When he emerged from the room, Mike said, "Don't ever come back here. There is about to be a raid."

"What? We come here once a week! What do you mean a raid? Mike, what aren't you telling me?"

"Look, Dee, I don't want you to know. The police can't get shit out of 'I don't know,' and that is the lane you need to stay in. You got it? Just don't go back."

He still reeked of onions and looked so worn out. He looked defeated. "Mike, I got it, but just tell me that you are okay."

He said, "Dee, as long as you are here and hold me every night despite the game, I can make it."

I leaned over to kiss him, and I felt love from him for the first time in a long time. It felt so good, until he touched my face and we were both sent tumbling back to our reality. I winced, and he began to cry. He apologized over and over again.

Then he said, "Dee, this shit is getting real. I brought that clown in, and now he is talking to the narcs. If you hadn't seen them, it would have been my ass. You saved my life tonight, babe—and to think I just put my hands on you. I love you. I am so sorry. I bit off more than I can chew, Dee. I just need you to be there."

By this time he was on his knees and crying into my stomach. I had to help him. "Baby," I cried, "we will figure this out together. I got your back."

I helped him up to his feet and took him to one of the spare rooms in the back, where I rode him like a new bike. It felt good to feel in control of things again. Sex was always the best way to clear the air for us. I wanted him to know what love felt like. I wanted him to feel good, and I wanted him to know that it was me doing the work.

He cried as he came and promised never to hit me again. We got dressed, tossed the sheets in the washer, and locked the door. Two days later, the raid made the front page of the paper. It seems that the cops found two kilos of cocaine in that apartment, but the guys just laughed. They knew they'd cleaned the apartment and the drugs were planted.

We hadn't gotten together since that night. All sales had been suspended. Nothing was moving. Errol was too paranoid. The streets were feeling it too. I heard Kat and Mike talking. They made the guy talking to the police break into the apartment for the onions.

I couldn't believe I was cheering for the bad guy. My, how my moral compass had changed, but it is amazing what you do for the ones you love.

Getting Real with the Ladies

We agreed to meet everyone at Club Gentleman. This was a good idea, because they had a private VIP room above the club. It allowed us to look down on and enjoy the crowd without being a part of it.

Errol and I arrived first, and he paid for the room and bartender. So he had literally just bought out the bar. And I was being forced to evaluate what was really going on around me. We had stopped hanging out at the apartment, and a few days later it was busted. Errol has been really low key since then. He barely went to the restaurant. That was unusual, too, but I was not ready to ask any questions yet. I thought that maybe if I waited a little longer, I could figure things out for myself.

They set up a couple of bottles on ice for the ladies at a table in the front of the room that overlooked the dance floor. Al poured five shots and left them on the bar. About this time, the door opened, and there were Kat, Black, Mike, Dee, and Lil Stupid.

For the first time in what seemed like forever, everyone was the same again. That family feeling filled the room. We were back.

I hugged Dee. Her face had healed, and she looked way happier than before. The guys were dapping each other up and laughing. They went to the bar, and Dee and I sat down at the table.

I could tell that she was uncomfortable around me. I could only think back to our last conversation.

I broke the silence. "Dee, did you see the bust on the news?"

"Yes."

"What the hell, Dee? Who are we dating?"

"Girl, you are dating the king of the Port City Kings."

I busted out laughing.

"What the hell, Clarke? What is so funny?"

"Girl, I am not surprised. Thanks for the confirmation."

Dee looked dumbfounded, but relieved and you could see it all over her face.

After that, the evening took a life of its own. Suddenly, I could appreciate my position. It felt good to look down on the city. I loved Dee, and I loved this new family of mine.

The guys were at the bar, laughing and arguing over the best rapper of all time. Jay-Z, Nas, Biggie, and Pac were all in the running. We had our guys back. No stress.

Dee said, "Clarke, who is that?" She pointed down to the floor, where two guys were clearing a path for a guy in a white suit. There were two guys in front of him and two behind him. They made their way to the stairs, and I looked over at Errol.

Suddenly I was afraid for my life. My hands were shaking, and my voice trembled as I said, "Hey, babe. Somebody is coming."

The door opened. Errol jumped up and moved quickly to the door. The two guys in front were the first to come to the door. They walked around Errol, and then I heard him yell.

In the blink of an eye, his hands were wrapped around the guy in the white suit. They dapped each other up and came into the room. They immediately walked to our table, and Errol introduced me. It was his brother, Admiral. He introduced me as his lady. I shot him a look, and he quickly added, "My one and only, my wifey." Then I could smile.

His brother kissed my hand, and the party began. Errol introduced Dee and Mike, and the drinks started to move. An hour later, the reggae was replaced with Eric Benet's "I Wanna Be Loved." It was midnight exactly.

Dee and I were laughing at the hood rats on the dance floor in their short skirts with their cups of water, when Errol patted me on my shoulder. I turned and he was on his knees.

As I looked at the diamond that sparkled in my face, I understood that he really meant it when he said he wanted this family forever.

"Clarke, you have changed my life, and I love you. Please don't make me live this life without you. Will you marry me?"

I screamed and jumped around, looking crazy, I'm sure—but the answer was yes. Emphatically yes. He smiled, and the room roared as I kissed my fiancé. Admiral tapped him on the shoulder and said, "Man, damn, give her the ring already."

It took up most of my finger. Yes, it was beautiful, but it was heavy.

We partied all night, and when the club closed, Errol thanked the guys for coming and opened the door.

Mike signaled to Dee that it was time to leave. I hugged her, then she and Mike followed Kat and Black down the stairs. Lil Stupid was already gone, and it was Errol, Admiral, Scott, and me.

I walked over to Errol and asked him if I should leave. He laughed and said, "Of course not, my love. You are welcome here and wherever I am."

It felt good to be welcomed and protected. Errol was so different from anyone else I'd ever dated. I was just glad to be around him. The puzzle pieces fit perfectly.

Admiral, Errol, and Scott and I were seated at the same table. Admiral took my hand and said, "My brotha has chosen you as his wife. This means that he trusts you. If you ever need me, call. " He kissed me on my cheek and was back to the bar, where he made small talk with his crew.

We ended the night with a toast to family. Then we exchanged more hugs and were on our way.

When I woke up the next morning, I offered to make breakfast for the crew, but Admiral was already gone. I called Dee, and she and Mike agreed to come over. It would be nice to have breakfast with a couple.

As we showered, Errol asked me questions about Mike and Dee. "Do you think Mike has a drug problem?"

"No. Dee said he is just stressed out. It has been hard for them since you cut their supply in half."

"How do you know about that?"

"You said it in front of me, remember? I play crazy, but I ain't. I don't speak unless spoken to."

He kissed me and said, "That's why I love you. So, what do you really think of Mike?"

"I think some people perform best when they have something to prove. Try him out and see. If he doesn't perform, it is what it is. I don't know a lot about him, but it would really help Dee out a lot. I speak more for her than him."

He didn't say anything else about Mike after that. He turned me around and picked me up. Everything was wet, and he slid in easily. He made my day, but messed up my hair. I didn't care, though.

I had just managed to dry my hair when Dee and Mike arrived. Errol was making breakfast as a peace offering for getting my hair wet. I got dressed in a loose pair of sweat pants and a T-shirt, and ran downstairs to meet our guests.

The table was set, and everyone was seated. Errol said the blessing and then he began the conversation that would change my life forever.

"Mike, I have heard that things have been tight around your house."

"Yes, Errol, it has been kinda rough since you cut my supply. I know I fucked up, man—but you can't punish me forever."

Errol threw down his napkin and said, "I can do whatever the fuck I want, but consider yourself lucky that I want to help your stupid ass. Don't let that mouth get you into trouble. This business is about what you don't say and do, not the other way around."

"Sorry, man. Thanks for looking out."

"Don't ever get it twisted. I meant what I said about Dee. She is a friend to Clarke, and if you ever touch her again, deals are off and lights go out. Am I clear?"

"Absolutely, man. Dee and I are fine. We love each other."

Errol looked at me and winked. Wow, I couldn't believe he took care of Dee for me. He did this to help her. I just hoped Mike wouldn't fuck up. I knew I had to talk to Dee.

That opportunity came soon enough when breakfast was done. Errol asked Mike to join him on the porch. That's where all the smoking went on and where the real deals were made. Dee asked me what was going on. I was only too happy to tell her that Errol was putting Mike back on.

Instead of her being happy, she was suddenly concerned. "I know you were just trying to help, Clarke, but Mike is using, and I am not sure how this is going to go. Errol has a reputation around this town, and I wouldn't want to find myself on the bad side of his temper because of some stupid shit Mike did."

"Talk to him, Dee. Get him some help and make him stop. If you don't think he can handle it, tell me and I will stop Errol."

"No, Clarke. He'll be fine. We got this. I'll help him. We need the money."

"Let me know, girl. I don't want no shit."

Dee said, "I will. Trust me, okay." But she sounded nervous and unsure, and suddenly I wasn't so sure I'd been a help to her at all.

Thick as Thieves

As time passed, Dee and I were inseparable. I knew she understood the life and didn't judge me. I didn't want random women around Errol, and I knew Dee had Mike. She was less of a threat. We had a few extra bedrooms, and many of our late-night drinking parties turned into sleepovers with Dee and me making breakfast the next morning.

Errol was beginning to give Mike more and more responsibility. And I could see things were changing for Dee. She traded her silver charm bracelet for a diamond tennis one. Things were good.

Errol and Mike were getting tight. And Kat and Black didn't like it too much. They felt Mike was taking their spot. He got more work and more love. Errol was beginning to come around less and less. Their once-a-week hangouts were reduced to once a month.

Errol had been gone so much lately. It was hard for me to keep up. One week it was Canada. Two weeks later, Jamaica. California a week after that. And Florida the month after. It was all a whirlwind.

By that time I was working longer hours so I could have something to do to break the monotony of the boring days while Errol was away.

Money came every Friday anytime Errol was gone. He would leave a checklist, and the funds would flow. Kat or Black would always bring it. No one else came to the house when Errol was away.

When Black came to make his drop one day, he was really tripping. "How can someone as rich as Errol be tied up with someone like you? You aren't Jamaican. You can't even cook for him."

"Shut up, Black. Make your drop and dip. You are drunk."

He leaped in my face, and that is when shit got real. "You think you all that since Errol got you that ring, but you still a hood rat. You are no better than the rest of the ass in the club." I backed up toward the desk on the side wall of the porch.

Black followed, staggering and saying, "You are trying to get him to cut us out. You and Dee and Mike are working together to push me out."

He hit himself on the chest and began to cry as he said, "I am the most loyal lieutenant. Why is Mike getting all this work? We want to eat too! This is all your fault, you hood rat bitch. You're gonna pay for this."

He took a step to get in my face, and I pulled my hand from the drawer, holding a pistol. "Nigga, you can start by getting outta my face before I drop your ass. Leave the money and dip while you still can."

He dropped the bag onto the floor and began to back away. "Clarke, I am so sorry. Please forgive me. Please don't tell Errol. I will do anything you ask. Please just don't tell Errol."

"You owe me, nigga. Now get the fuck outta my house."

He closed the door quietly behind him. I quickly locked it, my hands shaking. I was suddenly afraid. That was the first time I'd pulled a gun on anyone. I had no idea it wouldn't be my last.

I cried and shook as I called Errol and explained the situation. It was a bittersweet phone call for him. He couldn't believe I had handled myself that way. He was proud of me and told me I'd just graduated. He knew I knew where the guns were; he just never believed I'd have to use one of them.

He sent two guys from the restaurant to the house, and they stayed there for two days until he returned. They were his cousins, so it was like entertaining two big kids.

When Errol returned, I was in the kitchen making cookies, while the guys played Xbox. As he walked over to me, I saw the smile that made me love him.

He looked so relieved just to be home. He picked me up in the air and swung me around as Kat brought his bags in the door. Kat took the bags to our room and asked if there was anything else. Errol immediately responded, "Call Black."

I had no idea what Errol would do, but I was scared. The look I knew had been replaced by one I'd never seen. His eyes had turned hard and the light was gone from them.

I said, "Baby, I'm fine."

The look Errol shot me screamed at me to stay in my place. Kat sensed the tension and stepped outside. I had never seen Errol this serious before. He said, "I love you, and this is why I will excuse this. Disrespect comes at a price. I am the king, and you are my queen. He must be handled. Do you understand?"

"Understand what, baby? I pulled a piece on him. He was scared to death."

"Clarke, pulling a piece is only the beginning. What if he'd made you pull the trigger? I can't worry about you every time I leave."

I put my head down and said, "Errol, I don't mean to be a stress for you. It is obvious that you have enough on your plate." The tears began to fall. I couldn't hide them anymore. I couldn't look at him.

I ran upstairs and had just closed the door when he opened it behind me. He found me in the bathroom, crying and blowing my nose. The floodgates had fallen open.

"Errol, what the hell do you have me involved in? I agreed to love you, but I never signed up for all of this."

"I know, babe, I know. For that I am sorry. This is why I have been single for so long. It is hard to find someone who can love you through all of this, but I love you. I needed a woman who can handle my business. Clarke, that woman is you. I need you. I need you to help me run this thing from the sidelines. I need you to always have my back."

I shook my head and yelled, "Having your back means pillow talk and making you dinner every night. It doesn't mean getting shot or pulling guns on people. I want a fucking normal life. Do you hear me, Errol? I am done with this shit. I want a normal life."

"I don't have a normal life to offer you, Clarke. This is all I have to give right now. Will you trust me? Please, trust me with your heart. I will always protect it. Can you do that, Clarke? These vows are just as important as the ones we get from the priest. Do you understand? Can you love me anyway?" His eyes were full of water that began to run down his cheek as he begged me to love him.

He didn't need to; I loved this man, and even though he didn't know it, he'd given me the life I dreamed of. I blindly accepted. I was royalty in this world. I was staying. I loved my man and the family we were creating. I loved the bit of normalcy we'd been able to create amid all of this.

I was playing for keeps.

"Errol, I am not going anywhere. I am here. I love the family we've created."

His phone rang, and it was Kat. Black had just arrived. Errol told Kat to take him to the basement. I had no idea what that meant, but it didn't sound good.

"Baby, please don't hurt him. I've scared him enough."

"I know, Mafietta. Let me handle this. In the meantime, can you make me some lunch?" I had to smile as he smacked me on the behind then kissed me and walked away.

Mafietta. No one had called me that before, but it had a nice ring to it.

I was just pulling the fries from the grease when Black came through the kitchen with a freshly blackened eye. He apologized again and again for disrespecting me. Then he kissed my ring.

I wondered what the hell had just happened. I was still reeling when Errol and Kat followed and told him they'd call him later.

He seemed grateful when he left. I had no idea of Errol's real anger. I wouldn't know until later that I had saved Black's life.

Things were quiet after that. Errol started going back to the restaurant Monday through Saturday. The trips stopped, and we both went to work every day. The drops didn't come to the house anymore. When Errol came home, he was home. We didn't speak about anything that happened that summer. We found our shot at happiness and we took it. We were one happy family. We were beginning to plan our wedding, and business was booming.

Our engagement party was just what the group needed to rekindle the family feel. People are happy when they have money in their pocket, and our party was no exception. We received more money than I'd ever seen. Admiral was there with his wife, Sara. Kenny, Errol's older son, was in from France, and my family had rented a bus and come up from Charlotte.

A good time was had by all. I noticed the formation was back. Errol and I were always flanked with at least two people, who were always his cousins. The party was pretty open, and we were always covered in crowds. The same was true for Kenny. The family was to be protected at all times.

I loved Errol for this. We were not naive to the eventual consequences of our lifestyle and had contingency plans in place. He discussed them with me once, but they were never discussed again—just written and placed in a hidden safe under the floorboard.

There were people I'd never seen. Three Jamaican men who were also with guards were there. They brought their wives and families. Everyone loved food, so the families mingled well. The evening was full of good music, good liquor, and good people. The bus came to take the family back to their hotels, but the mother and father of each of the three Jamaican families stayed with us.

The kids were taken to the hotel with my family. Then another party started. Men began to take off blazers, only to reveal holsters filled with guns. It was time for me to go. This was too much for me. The ladies and I went into another living area to have a glass of wine.

We exchanged pleasantries, family photos, and wedding ideas. Everyone seemed trained to keep the conversation limited to trivial things. We spent the next two hours discussing shoes and handbags while our men were making moves to take over the city.

We ladies visited the restaurant for lunch the next day. Even though it is a restaurant, the women took over the kitchen. Those ladies taught me how to make my own beans, rice, and jerk chicken. It was a great day for me.

And as it turns out, it was a great day for Errol as well. His friends were the hidden hands, the real movers and shakers. Errol was really a king among the Kings. That is how they referred to each other as we enjoyed our food. The music was loud, and the bass was hitting. Sal, one of the Kings from the island, came from the kitchen with a tray of shots. His wife, Jean, came out with one filled with champagne flutes.

We partied for the next three days. And then our weekend was over. It was Tuesday and time to go back to the real world. The bus left, and the flights flew away. Finally, we were back to us.

We began to have these get-togethers at Marley Grill every Friday. I grew to look forward to them. We were a family again. Mike and Dee were doing well. She had a job and was pregnant. Black was always in my face, trying to see if I needed anything. I knew he was sorry and a true lieutenant, but he knew I was no joke and nothing to be played with.

Errol wanted to do something special for the guys, so he planned a weeklong trip to New Orleans for his team. I made all the arrangements. It was time to get away and enjoy life without all the eyes of the Port City on us and our shopping bags.

The Trip That Caused the Fall

Kat was the first to volunteer to stay back. He still felt the need to prove himself after all the authority Errol had given Mike, so we paid no attention to the request. Black was coming with us, and so were Lil Stupid, Dee, Mike, and Scott.

We flew first class. This was the first time for me, and it was nice not to have to pay for the headsets or alcohol. We were all feeling pretty good by the time we finally landed. We laughed and joked as we waited on our luggage. Once Black grabbed the last bag from the carousel, there was a limo waiting to take us to our hotel.

When we arrived, there was a message for Errol at the desk of our French Quarter Hotel. It simply said, "Two days," and was signed AB. As the two words hit him, I saw his legs go weak for a split second, but he quickly recovered. He folded the note and handed it to me. I put it in my purse, and we kept moving.

Once we'd tipped the attendant and the door was closed, he said, "Clarke, they're coming."

"Who's coming?"

"The cops."

"Why?"

"Kat."

"What?! Why would Kat do something like that?"

"He is too eager and far too impatient to be successful in this business. Loyalties are hard won, and he doesn't understand. His own ego will eat him alive. Admiral's wife warned me of this when she was here, but I assumed we had more time or that I could stop it from happening."

Back home, an underground connect was watching Kat as his shit fell apart. It seems he had too much to drink and decided to drive down Water Street. Hell, even I knew better than that. Water Street was always flooded with cops, because it was near the water front, but it had the best clubs. Kat got pulled with a quarter pound of weed and started singing like a bird. He had no idea that the cops didn't know who he was. He assumed he was more important than he was and ruined the game as we knew it.

Dumb ass.

I couldn't believe how quickly things were falling apart. Kat played the game so well. He should have been the first to know to keep his mouth closed. Loose lips sink ships, and ours seemed to be going down fast.

My next call was to Eric. I'd worked for him for years, and I knew he would help. I had more dirt on him than most, and he was a criminal attorney. Things seemed to fall in place. He would find out what was going on and get back to us.

We all had lunch as planned in the hotel restaurant. Errol was surrounded by those having fun, but he couldn't seem to partake of it himself. This broke my heart. We both knew what was coming; we couldn't prevent that, but it killed me that he wouldn't allow himself to enjoy this weekend.

I knew he had to meet with the guys, so I made the transition a little easier for him.

I said to Dee, "Let's let them chat it up, and we'll go to the spa. We need a day of relaxation. It takes a lot to love these guys." I kissed Errol and squeezed his hand as we made our way to the spa. Dee had no idea what was going on, and I couldn't tell her.

Errol explained nothing to his troops either. He decided against it. He didn't think they could handle it. He and I would handle it. I had Admiral's number and numbers of the wives of the three Kings. If I had a problem, I was to call Admiral and one of the wives. The rest would be decided, and I would be provided with instructions.

Errol didn't feel well that evening, so we stayed in as he gave the other couples a thousand dollars each to enjoy the city. I knew what was wrong. It wasn't his stomach; it was his heart. No one else understood what it was like growing up young, black, and poor, except his team. He didn't want that for his family or theirs.

The other side of that coin is the guilt of living a life that doesn't always allow you to look in the mirror. Finding a way to separate yourself from the bullshit you have done to survive sometimes eats people alive.

I held him for most of the evening in silence. We laughed as we watched *Pretty Woman*. Then I began to explain to him how he was my king. "Errol, I don't care what you do. I have always seen you to be a man of compassion. That is most important to me. We will get through the rest."

"I know they will try you."

"Don't worry, love. I have my own troops coming in. I can hold it down until you get back. Black will have my back behind them. We will be fine. There won't be a war until they start one. Baby, we got this."

"But, Clarke, can you love me regardless of the things I'm gonna have to do to get outta this?"

"Errol, this is forever. We're playing for keeps remember. Family first."

He managed a weak smile as a tear fell from his eye. "Family first."

The weight those words carried were the heaviest thing I've ever had to carry. I couldn't take them back or change them. I released them into the atmosphere, and I felt my spirit drop as Errol checked his email that day. There were two different gang-related shootings in the Port City that night. Kat and the rat from the apartment were dead. I watched him read the message, then he pushed his chair back, went to his CD case, and began to play Jay-Z's "Regrets."

The tears fell from his eyes as he said, "Babe, you need to learn this song. It will help you through. You can't be eaten by this life. You have to wield the sword when needed and always be the last to speak. I won't be gone long. They have no evidence; they can't hold me."

He had spoken with Eric, but neither of them shared a lot of details with me. For the first time in a long time, I wasn't sure of what was happening around me. I wanted to believe him, but his eyes held a dark secret. I knew there was a part of him I could never reach.

I held him all night. I don't think either of us slept at all, but there was no place for words. He felt like putty in my arms. I realized I was his strength right then. I had his back, and he trusted me. I would hold him down and get to the bottom of this. Someone would answer, or the streets would feel my wrath.

We made the most of our last two nights in New Orleans. Errol began to loosen up as he realized the importance of the moments we had left together. I think he knew that these last moments would be the ones that held and encouraged me while he was away. These memories would be the ones to keep me company while he was gone.

We were all smiles as we saw the characters of Bourbon Street. Dee and I were amazed by Ashley, the Traffic Trani, as she directed traffic on the cross street of Bourbon. Errol was initially shocked by what he called the Batty Boy, but at the same time was humored by her outrageous antics. Her show amazed the throngs of people crossing to the rainbow side of Bourbon Street, and the dollars attached to her G-string proved it. Dee and I gave her a hundred each, and she blew her whistle, slid on the top of a cab, and gave a show that caused Errol, Black, and the crew to leave us standing there alone in the crowd.

We spent the last night bar hopping and taking a carriage ride through the French Quarter before returning to our hotel. Our trip started off rocky, but we found a way to make the best of it. Time was of the essence now. Errol and I had tons to discuss.

He wanted to make sure I was protected and wanted to call in a crew from home. I knew my cousins could handle it. After I explained to him how things were done in the country, he was sure of it too.

My cousins from back home would arrive an hour before us and wait at the airport until we landed. I knew my family was bout it. Now Errol did too. I just never told them about Errol. Today was the day to break that silence. I needed them.

After reaching the baggage claim, I saw two familiar faces. My cousins Arvin and Rocko sped up to greet me— Arvin was more stocky than tall, but nobody messed with him. Rocko was so cool, he could reason with anyone. I would be left in a pretty cool balance between them. Being without Errol wouldn't be so bad if they were there.

The two days passed quickly. Errol spent much of that time getting things in order and making lists. He chatted with his son Kenny quite a bit and left him with very simple instructions. He was to behave as he would if he were home. My word was his word, and that word was final. This was the message to family within and family without. He asked Kenny to pass the word to Admiral.

It was the second day since we'd been back, and I'd pretty much gone underground since the trip. My days had been filled with hundreds of questions and what-if scenarios. Arvin and Rocko were brought up to speed. They couldn't believe what kind of man their cousin was about to marry, and they were mad that I hadn't told them sooner.

Errol and I took a shower as usual that morning, but he seemed too weak to even bathe himself. I rubbed soap on his strong back and told him, "Errol, you can handle this. We know what to do. I will make sure you have what you need until we get you home. The streets will take care of the streets."

Now it was his turn to ask me all the what-if questions. The only consolation to the decisions I had to make was that song, "Regrets." It was now in my playlist.

I massaged every muscle in his body. He tried to fight the urge to relax, but he could not. He threw his head back against the shower wall and enjoyed the moment.

When it passed, I lathered him up and washed him again. We got dressed and held each other until 11 a.m. We knew that was when they would come.

The cops seemed disappointed as they found our door open; there was no chance to use their battering ram. They explained they were there to execute a search warrant, and we were happy to comply. They didn't find anything, but asked to take Errol downtown for questioning. He didn't resist, but asked me to call Eric.

It was happening. It was time to activate the plan. It was time for me to live my dream. Errol turned to kiss me. I hugged my fiancé, kissed him once more, and watched him walk out of the door.

I called Black and asked him to schedule a meeting at the warehouse in the country. I pulled the written instructions from the safe to present to Errol's lieutenants. These instructions explained the line of succession while he was away. I was hopeful, despite the fact that I knew this wouldn't be easy. Arvin and Rocko were there for support, and each of them flanked my sides as I took a seat at the head of the table at our meeting that night.

This floored Mike. He was immediately upset that he was not chosen to follow as leader. His shit started before the meeting could.

"Who gave you the right to sit in that chair? Just because you pulled a gun on Black doesn't mean we are afraid of you or we have to do what you say. We will do things the way we did when Errol was here, and I'll make a drop to you every Friday. That's it, Clarke. We mean it!"

"Who is *we*," I asked.

The room was quiet. Mike stood up and said, "I speak for all of us."

"Again, who is *all of us*? I need to see who us is."

Two cousins joined him. It broke my heart to see the family split, but regret was part of the game. I asked the three of them to remain standing as I read Errol's wishes. They were simple: respect her word and abide by it as if it were my own. No questions or exceptions.

I appealed to Mike. "Do you understand the instructions of your king?"

"Yes."

"And what say you now?"

"I say, things will be the same—"

Before he could finish, the room fell silent as a bullet shot by his ear. I asked again, and his voice trembled as he said, "Like I said, things will be the same." Suddenly a second shot rang out, and blood dripped from the hole in his head.

The entire room seemed to gasp for breath at the same time.

I was too afraid to tremble. "Now, is there anyone else who wants to challenge Errol's words? This is the last time you niggas are gonna get my hands dirty. Do you understand?"

The room fell silent. Then I said, "Everything will be the same as it was when Errol was here, but instead of Mike, Black, will you do me the honor of making the drops, and Scott, will you call in a cleaner?"

I had no idea what exactly a cleaner did. Errol just told me to call a cleaner if I had the need to shoot someone. Glad I didn't forget that tidbit of information, even though I thought he was crazy for telling me that three days ago.

"Now, if you'll excuse me, gentlemen, I think your instructions are clear." Arvin pulled back my chair, and Rocko held the door.

As soon as it was closed, I barely made it to the trash can on the opposite wall before I was spewing up my dinner. It was the first time I'd ever pulled a trigger. I had taken something that I couldn't give back. I was destined for fire and brimstone. In this world, this action was necessary, but in the real world—the normal one—this was some messed-up stuff.

Arvin rubbed my back as I held on to the trash barrel for life. Then I felt my knees get weak. I collapsed. I had shot a nigga, thrown up, and fainted. I had run a long way from the little girl in the Starlighter choir who made speeches at Sunday school conventions. I was a killer. I still loved the Lord as much as before, and I knew he would protect me, but I didn't trust these guys anymore. Errol wasn't there and I could only lean on what I knew. I could only trust those who knew me and would always put my best interests first.

From that point forward, I would only see Black, Arvin, or Rocko. There was no need to see anyone else. Dee had been leaving messages on my phone for days. Mike hadn't come home, and she was really worried.

How in the hell could I tell her I just killed her man for disrespecting me. I couldn't. I wouldn't. I hit the ignore button and went back to reading the paper.

We sent Errol money every week, and I visited online three times a week. Black visited twice a week, and Kenny, the other two days. We wanted to make his days in jail fly by. The lawyers were throwing all these technical terms in my face, but they all seemed to cover up the fact that they were really holding him on some bullshit. Eric would sort through it, though.

On a brighter note, the money was always on time, and everyone was eating. No one came to my house anymore. Arvin and Rocko were running the restaurant, and I decided who they served. If you were short, pissed me off, or were suspect, we didn't deal with you. I was very selective.

I also didn't deal with people who were too eager or came off as know-it-alls. I respected the silence of the game. Power had a look, and if you didn't have it, Marley Grill didn't serve you. If you sold near schools, we didn't serve you. If you beat up on your baby moms, we didn't serve you. No one talked to me, and I liked it that way.

I was running by the Grill one Friday when I met Dee waiting for me beside my car. Her hair was matted, and she obviously hadn't showered in days. She was hysterical. She began to cry and scream in the street that someone has killed Mike.

"What?" was all I could manage.

"Why would you think that?"

"He hasn't been home in a week, Clarke."

I know this was cruel, but I had to say something. "Have you checked his baby's momma's house?"

"Yes, Clarke. I called her. He isn't there. No one has seen him. Not his mom or his sister or the streets. He is missing, Clarke. I haven't seen him since he left for that meeting. Did you see him?"

"Yes, Dee. He was there, but I am not sure where he ended up after."

At least this part was true. A guy came with tools and tons of cleaning supplies. I didn't ask any questions. Scott was there to pay him, so I really don't know.

I stood in the street and held her as she cried in my arms. I saw the cousins watching me from the restaurant with somber faces. They knew the story, but they would never breathe it to anyone. In that instance, I knew they felt sorry for me. How could I have love for her after murdering her old man?

I wasn't sure, but I did. I still wanted the best for her, and I knew she was probably struggling with things since Mike hadn't been around to help out with things. I had to help her, and things were too volatile to leave her alone. I had to keep her with me.

Dee loved to do hair and makeup, and she was very good at it. So she kept me looking hot. She tidied things up around the house and quickly became my personal assistant.

With Dee around, I was virtually untouchable. She helped me expand the business even further. Soon we were delivering to most of the major employers. We would add something special in their lunch orders on every payday. This was working. We were surprised to find out who gets high.

The beauty of it is that Dee and I never had to show our faces. Business had nearly doubled because of the new corporate additions. We were barely keeping up with the demand and having to contract some of it out to other parts of the family.

Dee needed help running the business, and we'd found a better way to do things. The men were the enforcers while the women ran things behind the scenes. We worked out where, when, and how much, and they delivered. There were even circles where women were running things in the Port City.

When Dee initially suggested that we bring Tina on, I was a bit hesitant. I didn't need someone else I had to watch. I needed to look at her; I could size her up in seconds. So I told Dee to bring her in on Tuesday. I was going to make the bank deposit that day. Money was coming so fast that we had to make three deposits a week at four different banks.

I didn't want Tina touching my money, and Dee insisted she could help in other ways. I was behind the bar, grabbing a pineapple soda, when Tina walked in for her interview. She was much smaller than when

I saw her last. Her face looked tired. She was dressed neatly enough, but no name-brands or bling. When she opened her mouth to speak to me, I knew she had a story, and I wanted to know what it was.

I needed the facts, but I didn't have time to filter through the bullshit, so I said, "I know you are here to make money, but I need someone who *needs* to make money. I don't have time to babysit. What is your story? You have five minutes."

She began to tell her painful story. She was like so many other sisters looking for love in all in the wrong places. I listened as she began.

She had spent the last of her small paycheck from the department store where she worked to buy a pair of high heels that she could barely walk in and a new dress that hugged every curve and showed every last bit of cleavage.

Her home girl had come over and began the painful process of braiding down her natural hair to sew in the rows and rows of weave she had in a bag in the top of her closet. After the dress, shoes, thongs, new bra, and hair, she was broke. She couldn't even buy herself a drink in the club, but she was determined to be there. She was convinced that the rest would take care of itself.

And that it did.

The night began simply enough. She and her home girl headed out to College Night. They were both tired of being alone. The free drinks flowed all night, and the guys were everywhere.

There was a particular group of guys that caught their attention. They seemed to be different from all the other guys. They weren't surrounded by females, and they were all well-dressed. They stood tall, and the young ladies quickly noticed the Polo, Nautica, and Izod emblems they were all wearing. The game was on.

For a while, their grinding captivated their pack's attention, but then the guys wanted more. The two young ladies had a choice to make, for they had been invited to a "private" after-party. One young lady immediately refused, while the second stood there thinking.

She knew these guys. She knew what they represented. They were all from predominate families, and worst-case scenario, they could afford it. She was willing to take her chances. Her friend urged her not to stay, but her mind was fixed, and her friend finally relented. They were beginning to make a scene, anyway.

The ladies exchanged a brief hug and one went home alone, the same way she'd come. The other found herself in the back seat of a Tahoe. She knew she was drunk, so she couldn't figure out where all the hands were coming from. The world was spinning, so she knew she was tripping.

She couldn't remember which one of the smiling faces removed her shoes or her dress. Everything was a blur. She felt something, and she liked it. This guy had it going on. Then things got dark and the feeling changed. It was a different feeling, still somewhat pleasurable, but different. She managed to open her eyes, and even the guy looked different. She thought he was lighter than this, but she couldn't get past the haze in her head. Everything was so cloudy and mixed up, and the room was still spinning, so she closed her eyes to enjoy the moment.

She woke up as some unfamiliar face tossed her dress at her. She didn't even remember this guy. She looked around, and there were two guys lying across the bed in their boxers, while she was completely naked.

She tried to remember what happened to her, but it was all a blur. She asked this kind stranger if he knew what had happened, and he laughed and tossed her his phone. Her heart fell to her stomach as she pressed the play button.

Tears streamed from her eyes as she dropped the phone on the floor. She jumped into her dress, and it didn't matter to her that it was inside out or that her weave was tangled and wet. There was a used condom stuck to one of her shoes. She removed it and tossed it on one of the limp bodies lying on the bed.

She asked this unfamiliar face to show her to the bathroom. There she managed to adjust her clothing and get that sticky stuff out of her hair. The silence was deafening, and she had to leave. This place was choking her, and it was all she could do to fight back the rest of her tears.

The unfamiliar face only spoke to her once and that was to ask for her address. As soon as she turned her key and stepped inside her apartment, the damn burst and the tears came. They burned her face as they fell. She was embarrassed and empty.

Her friend rushed to the living room to inquire of her night. But as soon as she saw her friend's face, she knew words were not necessary. They held each other, and they cried together. She just wanted to have a good time. She just wanted to feel loved. She had hoped to fill the emptiness she carried so deep inside of her.

And she had—just not the way she thought. When the blood didn't come, she knew that her life would forever be changed. She'd been hit by a train that she never saw coming.

I felt sorry for Tina. I wasn't so different from her. A part of me wanted to judge and dismiss her, but Tina needed to work to provide for her daughter. She never tried to find her daughter's father, because she was so embarrassed by the situation. She was ridiculed by her family, and her mom threw her out because she couldn't pay the rent anymore.

This could have been me. She was brave enough to have her daughter. When I was faced with pregnancy at the age of seventeen, I was not woman enough to make that move and ended up on the table at the clinic.

I had to help this young lady. I agreed to bring her on, but told Dee to show her the ropes. She understood my zero tolerance for stupid, but was up to the challenge. I liked this little girl. I gave her four hundred dollars and told her to pick up some clothes for her and her daughter.

"Dee," I said, "keep her out of my sight until you figure out what to do with her."

"I won't be any trouble, Ms. Clarke. I promise."

"You'd better not, sugar. Your life depends on it."

Legends

Dee and Tina took me at my word, and before long we had relationships with local barbershops, beauty shops, mom and pops, and gambling joints. Our quantities were doubling, and it was hard to keep up with the demand. I liked the money associated with it, but the risk was making me uncomfortable. I didn't want this traced back to us.

We were putting out at least one hundred kilos a week. We could have moved more, but the shipments Errol arranged before leaving forced us to make side deals with other teams. Our cousins were always glad to see us and showed us a tremendous amount of love, but these were Scott's people. They loved Errol, but they didn't know me. They were respectful enough, but preferred to handle business with Scott. They were afraid of handling me wrong. They knew I didn't take disrespect lightly, and they knew Errol wouldn't either.

Errol still called quite a few shots from behind bars, and even though he was on forced vacation, he was still king of the Port City.

I decided it was time to call Admiral to renegotiate. "Hello, my brother-in-law."

"Hello, Clarke. How are you?" He seemed surprised to hear my voice.

"Thank you for the money you sent this month, but could you send double next week?"

"Double?"

"Yes, Admiral. Expenses have grown since Errol has been away, and I need to meet our obligations."

To anyone else it would have sounded like Admiral was sending money to help us get by since Errol was locked up, but I was asking Admiral to double my coke supply that week. I needed two hundred kilos. I knew I could move at least 150 kilos of it and the other fifty could sit in the floor safe in the storage room. The money was coming so fast. We had to constantly come up with ways to make it all look legal.

Errol had to admit that building the floor safe and fake room in our storage facility had been a great move for us. The opportunity to buy the building had fallen in our lap. One of Errol's soldiers fell on hard times and sold us the entire place for four kilos of coke. We owned an acre of land on the lot behind the storage units. It was surrounded by a natural barrier of twelve-foot-tall pine trees. I didn't think that was enough, so I had a ten-foot privacy fence installed two feet inside the tree line. Arvin and Rocko hooked it up like a cow fence in the country; if you touched it . . . let's just say you were in for quite a shock.

We bought twenty U-Haul trucks of all sizes and a wrecker service. That business did fairly well on its own. But most importantly, it made my hands look clean. Whenever we brought loads in, we would use our wreckers to pick up what looked like abandoned cars—filled with pure cocaine. If we were ever stopped, we didn't know anything. All we needed was reasonable doubt. That wouldn't be a problem.

I didn't speak to Errol about my exploits in his absence. He just knew everything was good. He got all his news from Rick, who was a guard at the local sheriff's department. From time to time, Rick would deliver handwritten notes and home-cooked meals to Errol. The notes cost me three hundred dollars each, and dinners were five hundred. I didn't care. Errol would have what he needed. That was what mattered to me.

Errol was worried about the risk I was taking. I was doing numbers in the Port City that he was seeing in cities like Raleigh and Charlotte. I knew he didn't want me to end up like him, but we were running the city. Life was good, and there was no reason to look back. Everyone was making money, and it was coming so fast we could all be legit in a matter of months.

I didn't go to the restaurant or the towing office anymore. I could handle everything remotely. Arvin handled the restaurant, and Rocko handle the storage and towing. I spent my time volunteering at Randy's school and in the community. I never attended civic functions, but I was always a major contributor. I knew the city, and it knew me. I wanted to keep it that way. I wanted to be aware of the radar, while staying under it.

We were doing well, but it was time to call a meeting.

Change Is in the Air

I never knew how hard it would be for Clarke to come visit me. I couldn't hug, kiss, or caress her with this plastic window between us. I was afraid of all the encounters she would tell me about. I knew she was okay, but probably facing a hard time, and I could just imagine what it was like to have my partners treating my turf as if it was their own. There had to be an end in sight, even if I couldn't see it. She had no idea how rough it could get. Hell, I really didn't either.

There was an old cat in here that peeped me out and schooled me real quick on the ins and outs of the jail. After a couple of hard-won victories in the game of chess, I knew which guards and prisoners I could pay to make things happen for me. I didn't want any trouble, but I refused to be a marked man in here.

All of these things were running through my mind as Clarke sat down before me. Surprisingly enough, I had no time to tell her my discoveries. She had gone into crisis mode and began talking herself. She told me not to worry and that everything was fine. I asked her about the family, and she told me she'd had some issues with one of my children, but it was handled and home was great. She said things were running smoothly.

The first true smile in months filled my face as she told me of how well things were going. She told me the wrecker service was booming. She was very careful as she spoke, but told me to rest assured that things would be fine when I got back.

For the first time, I could almost breathe. The Kings did not take kindly to weakness, and I couldn't let on to anyone how weak and helpless I felt. Clarke knew me; she saw the water filling my eyes, and she put her hand up as if to stop the dam of water from spilling over. She blew me a kiss, told me to enjoy my dinner, and told me she loved me as she walked away.

I must admit that I felt a little confused and dismissed as she left. Did she have any idea of what the food was like? I didn't even get to tell her about all the connections I'd made in here. How did I forget everything? I was furious with myself. I was taken back to my cell, but was surprised to hear my name called a couple of hours later.

I was taken to a dimly lit room, and my heart began to race as I ran potential scenarios through my head. I wondered who was going to be waiting in the dark corner of that room and how hard I would have to fight for my life.

Instead of a prisoner emerging, I saw a guard point to a small table in the dark corner. What the hell did a guard want with me? Once I made my way to the table, it was all so clear. I broke down as I saw a plate of jerk chicken with rice and peas before me. Beside that were a fork and a cell phone.

The guard said, "You have twenty minutes," and he was out of the door. I had no idea what Clarke meant when she said she had it handled, but then I knew why I loved her so much. My first call was to her disposable cell. She picked up on the first ring.

She answered by saying, "I love you."

"I love you, too," I replied.

She gave me the rundown on the things that had been happening—even her issue with Mike. It broke my heart to see her get her hands dirty. Clarke knew the business, but she never touched the business, and that was the way I wanted to keep it, but she went mafietta on the guys.

She was running a tighter ship than I ever did. She had turned trouble season into double season. I was proud of her. There was plenty of money on my books, and I gave her a list of people to send money to inside. This would ensure my protection.

I was proud of her, and things were going well. Just then I heard a knock on the door, and suddenly my moment of freedom was over. I ended my call, deleted the number, and was taken back to reality. I spent the evening thinking of how I would reclaim my throne when I was out of here. Then things could go back to normal. Clarke would be out of the business, and I would be back to head up the family. She could run the towing company, hair salons, and barber shops, and I could handle the rest. We would be even richer than before.

There were no outs in this life. We were here to stay!

Time to Put Down My Stiletto

Biggie had the "More Money, More Problems" concept down, and the problem was slapping me in the face—literally. The money was beginning to come in so fast, it was hard to hide it all. Do you know what it's like trying to tell someone coming from nothing to invest their money? Their spending was getting ridiculous, and it was time for a meeting. I didn't need that kind of attention.

Dee and Tina took a lot of the stress off me. Having Dee and Tina run the beauty and barber shops tripled my income within three months. Everyone gets a haircut; it doesn't matter where they work or how much money they make, and they love for women to do it. So they learned how to fit in with men.

They were always eager to sit down and tell me about their experiences. We conducted tons of business, but we only saw each other on Thursdays. We still called it ladies night. I was beginning to notice more and more tinted Tahoes and Suburbans around lately. It was time to tighten up.

Gage had just gotten locked up. I never met him, but I'd spent tons of his money on a regular basis. He was busted with enough shit to make me uncomfortable. From then on, things would be different. If you wanted to deal with the Bellows, you would be required to have a way to explain it or an accepted plan to hide it. The money would flow either way, and for me it was time to prune the hedges.

I had not attended a meeting since I shot Mike. I didn't want to see their faces. I didn't want to look in their eyes and see what was hidden behind the smiles they paraded in front of me as they shook my hand and tried to make conversation.

There is a circle of life in the streets, just like in that Disney movie. The top guy takes over the little guy's turf, and then for some reason or another he gets killed or arrested, and then the little guys have their turf back. I had seen it on every episode of any gangster show real or fake. The bad guy always loses. I didn't want that for us.

I didn't care so much what outsiders thought of our lifestyle anymore. I knew the people who surrounded me. I knew their children and their parents. We were a family, and we protected each other. This meeting would separate the group. I knew this, and it was okay. We wanted money and we had it. We wanted businesses and we had them. We wanted homes and we owned them. This was the seed. This was the goal.

Now it was time to fish. Make it look legal or get out of the Kings was the ultimate message.

The stress of it all was beginning to be more than I wanted. Too many people were depending on the decisions I made and Errol was depending on me to make sure he was taken care of inside. This was always mission number one for me.

When Errol and I talked, he had good news. If no evidence was provided in the next twenty-four hours, he would have to be released. I felt better than I had in a long time. Our conversations about the outside family had recently been limited to one-word responses. He would ask how the family was and I would reply, "Good."

And I would tell him about our family. He knew very little about the new ventures, and up until then I always felt he would be happy, but I couldn't be sure right now.

I was making triple the money he made before they took him months before. This really gave me a chance to do some legit shit with it. With all our new ventures, we still netted over one hundred thousand a month legally. This was good enough for me.

I had become a *boss*, a real mafietta, but I knew time was winding down for us if we didn't change our tactics. Errol would be home soon, and all he had to do was enforce the changes. We would finally be legit, and our lives could change forever.

An Excerpt From

Mafietta

Part II

A House Divided

A House Divided

Some people get in the game to better themselves. Those are the ones who make enough money to roll it into something legit and then bail. Others are in it for the hood credit that comes along with it. It was never about the fame for me. It was always about the bottom line and staying out of jail.

Jail sentences weren't kind to families. It tested their strength and resolve. I'd held Errol down the entire time he was away while keeping our name off the radar. I could not fathom how or why he would want to come home and pick up where he left off.

If he wanted to pick up with me, it would have to be real and it would have to be legit. I'd become well respected in our community, and I was finally able to hold my head up after the incident with Mike. No one ever found him, and I left the weight of that at the altar one Sunday morning long ago.

This was not a lifestyle I wanted for my family and definitely not for my children. Errol had no idea that I was pregnant, and I had no desire to tell him now.

Our last few conversations were filled with his dreams for the family despite the harm they could put us in. All of my work had been for nothing. I couldn't go back to that lifestyle. We had a chance to get out, and he refused to take it.

It's a good thing I kept my apartment, because for now, we stood *a house divided.*